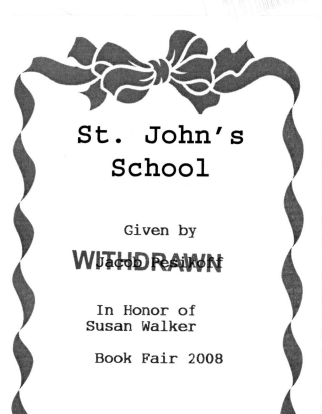

St. John's
School

Given by
Jacob Pesikoff

In Honor of
Susan Walker

Book Fair 2008

THE
ATTACK OF THE FROZEN WOODCHUCKS

THE ATTACK OF THE FROZEN WOODCHUCKS

BY

Dan Elish

ILLUSTRATIONS BY Greg Call

LAURA GERINGER BOOKS
An Imprint of HarperCollinsPublishers

The Attack of the Frozen Woodchucks
Text copyright © 2008 by Dan Elish
Illustrations copyright © 2008 by Greg Call

Library of Congress Cataloging-in-Publication Data
Elish, Dan.
    The attack of the frozen woodchucks / by Dan Elish ; illustrations by Greg Call. —
1st ed.
        p.   cm.
    Summary: When extraterrestrial woodchucks attack, ten-year-old Jimmy, his two-
and-a-half-year-old sister, friend William, and an eccentric classmate who has built a flying saucer in her Manhattan brownstone join forces to save the universe.
    ISBN 978-0-06-113870-6 (trade bdg.) — ISBN 978-0-06-113871-3 (lib. bdg.)
    [1. Extraterrestrial beings—Fiction. 2. Interplanetary voyages—Fiction.
3. Woodchuck—Fiction. 4. New York (N.Y.)—Fiction. 5. Science fiction.
6. Humorous stories.]   I. Title. II. Call, Greg, ill.
PZ7.E4257Att 2008   2006102962
[F]—dc22   CIP
                                                                      AC

Typography by Carla Weise
1 2 3 4 5 6 7 8 9 10

First Edition

Table of Contents

ONE

The First Sighting

As Jimmy Weathers helped his mother set the table that Saturday evening in early April, he had no idea that the fate of mankind was about to come crashing down on his shoulders. It happened just as Jimmy was laying a fork on his father's napkin. The front door to his family's small two-bedroom apartment burst open. In ran Imogene, Jimmy's two-and-a-half-year-old sister.

"Woodchuck, Mommy!" she cried, pulling hard on Jimmy's mother's pants. "Big, giant woodchuck!"

Jimmy smiled. He and Imogene shared a small room. He was very used to what he called "Genie-speak."

Jimmy's mother scooped Imogene into her arms.

"A woodchuck? Tell Mommy where you saw it."

The girl flung her purple backpack onto the sofa. "In park!"

The boy saw the smile curling on his mother's lips. Whatever Imogene had thought she had seen, it most certainly had *not* been a woodchuck. With the exception of squirrels, mice, and pigeons, New York City's Central Park was not known for its wildlife. He doubted there had been a woodchuck there for a hundred years, let alone a "giant" one.

"Now, now, dear," Jimmy's mother said. "Are you sure it was a woodchuck you saw?"

Before Imogene had a chance to answer, Jimmy's father was in the room, eyes wide. He laid the day's mail on the dining-room table and began waving his arms. His whole being took on a wild, excited glow.

"The largest darned one you ever saw, Emma!"

Jimmy and his mom exchanged a smile. By day Richard Weathers was a lawyer at the firm of Weasel, Waxel & Whine—a job he hated. By night he was a frustrated children's novelist who had written an entire shelf's worth of unpublished books, often animal-themed, with titles that ranged from *Chickens Who Tango* to *The Sloth Who Ruled Europe*. One of Jimmy's favorites included a character with unusual dining habits, who began each meal with a special poem:

I eats the feets of fried raccoon—
I eats them with a three-pronged spoon.
Dinner comes, my day's complete
Chompin' on them raccoon feet.

Indeed, Jimmy and his mom—and really all of Richard Weathers's friends—were used to the ramblings of his overactive imagination. A giant woodchuck? Jimmy didn't bat an eye.

"Oh, really, Dad?" the boy said, playing along. "How big was he?"

Jimmy's father jumped up on one of the foldout chairs they used in the dining room and stretched his arms all the way to the ceiling.

"Big!" he said. "We're talking twenty, thirty feet!"

"Big, big woodchuck!" Imogene said.

Jimmy's father hopped back to the floor and kept on talking. "It was unbelievable. There I was, watching Imogene playing in the field by the playground, when all of a sudden she decides to run after a squirrel. Naturally I follow. Soon we find ourselves in woods up around 103rd Street. No one was around. That's when we saw it."

"The woodchuck?" Jimmy asked.

"No," his father said, unzipping his coat. "The giant pod!"

Jimmy's mother was serving the spaghetti by now. Pasta was a family favorite.

"Oh, of course," she said, winking at Jimmy. "Like a giant dinosaur egg, I imagine."

"Egg!" Imogene said. "Like in museum."

"Exactly," her father said, rubbing a hand through his daughter's hair. "Just like at the natural history museum." He looked back up at his wife and son. "But when this puppy hatched, it was no Stegosaurus that came out. No, not at all! The egg split, and there it stood—a three-foot-tall woodchuck—completely frozen!"

"Frozen?" Jimmy said. He had to admit he was enjoying the story, one of his father's better ones. "Why was it frozen?"

His father looked disappointed. "Jimmy! Jimmy!" he said, rubbing his son's shoulders. "Don't you remember last week's blizzard? For all we know, that egg was sitting there through the storm."

Jimmy nodded. It was true—New York City had been bombarded by a series of blizzards that winter. Still, over the last few days the weather had finally begun to warm up. It seemed that spring was on its way at last.

"And here's what I think," his father went on. "It was the warmer weather that made it happen."

"Made what happen, dear?" Emma asked.

Jimmy's father looked from his son to his wife, eyes glinting. "Made that woodchuck thaw out and grow!"

With that, Imogene jumped as high as she could, stretched her arms over her head, and shouted, "Grow and grow and grow, grow, grow!"

"All right, dear," Jimmy's mother said, scooping Imogene into her booster seat. "We get the point. Dinner, everyone."

"So what did you do then, Dad?" Jimmy asked, sitting down. "I mean, about this thirty-foot woodchuck?"

His father blinked. "Do? Why Imogene and I did what you or any sane, self-respecting person in the world would have done. First we screamed. Then we ran for it!"

"Stroller motor!" Imogene announced. "Zoom!"

Jimmy and his mother smiled. A week earlier his father and Imogene had attached a toy motor to her stroller. While the motor didn't make the stroller go any faster, it did cough up an impressive amount of dust from the city sidewalks.

"So wait a second," Jimmy said, turning to his dad. "You mean there's still a giant, possibly man-eating, woodchuck at large in Central Park? Like right across the street?"

Despite their smallish apartment, Jimmy and his family were lucky to live just off the park.

His father nodded. "That's right. I stopped a policeman on the way home, but he didn't want to hear about it."

Again Jimmy saw his mother smile, but this time there was a trace of worry. This wasn't the first time his father had come home spinning an outrageous tale. A short week earlier, his subway car had been driven by a giant purple squid; a week before that, Hank, the building's doorman, had magically transformed into a tap-dancing sea lion. In both instances Jimmy's mom had laughed along with the rest of them. On the other hand, the boy had also overheard enough late-night conversations between his parents to know that, while his mom fully supported his father's writing, she was impatient for him to focus a little bit more on his real career. Apparently Jimmy's father had taken to staying home until ten or sometimes eleven in the morning to work on his books before heading to the office. Recently he had accidentally distributed a rough draft of one of his stories around his office. On the morning in question, the senior partners of Weasel, Waxel & Whine had opened their e-mail expecting to find a legal brief, only to come upon the opening pages of *The Porpoise Who Climbed Kilimanjaro*. "As sea creatures went," his father had written, "Hilma was a porpoise with a purpose."

"Anyway," Jimmy's dad went on, swallowing a mouthful of water, "after dinner I'm going down to the police station to register a formal complaint."

Jimmy saw his mother's face cloud over. For a moment he thought she was going to say something like "Richard? Isn't that taking things a little too far?" After all, making up a tale of a giant woodchuck was one thing. But actually reporting it to the police? That was crazy. But just then Imogene decided to experiment with hurling her pasta across the room to see if it would stick to the Van Gogh print on the wall. After order had been restored, Jimmy changed the subject. For the rest of the meal, the family focused on more ordinary matters: the Mets season opener and Jimmy's view that his school assigned far too much homework. All thoughts of giant frozen woodchucks were cast aside.

After plates were cleared, Jimmy watched his daily ration of TV while Imogene sat on the living-room floor, using a PlayStation tool kit to pry open the back of an old Game Boy. One of Jimmy's.

"I fix it," she said.

Jimmy didn't object. Ever since she had helped their father rig her stroller motor, Imogene had her hands into everything mechanical. Besides, the Game Boy hadn't worked for months.

"Thanks, Genie."

"I make it turn on TV," the girl said with a determined nod.

Jimmy just smiled. Why not let her try? Soon, though, his mother hustled her off to bed. A while later, when Jimmy's show ended, he felt his father's hand on his shoulder.

"Want to take a walk with me, Jim?"

Usually the offer of an after-dinner walk was a no-brainer. But to his surprise, Jimmy found himself hesitating. Yes, it was unlikely, but what if his father really *was* going to the police? Jimmy didn't think he could bear to see the look on the sergeant's face when his father rushed in, breathless, and demanded that a squad be dispatched to the park to search for a giant killer rodent.

"Think I'll pass this time, Dad," Jimmy said. He patted his math textbook. "Homework."

"On a Saturday night?" his father asked. "Okay. Suit yourself."

Moments later he was gone. Though Jimmy tried to concentrate on long division, he found his mind wandering back to his father's story. When a light breeze ruffled the living-room curtains, Jimmy jumped, half expecting to see the long whiskers of a giant woodchuck poking into the room. A short time later, his worksheet finished, Jimmy headed to his parents' room to say good night to his mother, who was seated at an oak desk, peering at the computer screen. Jimmy knew that she was going over the spreadsheets for Emma's Tea, her small shop down the block on 100th Street and Columbus Avenue. Though Jimmy's mother had a number of loyal customers, it was nearly impossible to sell enough cups of tea and muffins to support a family in New York City—even one in a small two-bedroom apartment. Still, there she was, trying to see if there was any way for her little corner store to bring in more money. When Jimmy knocked on the door, she quickly reduced the screen so he couldn't see.

"Night, Mom."

"Night, dear." She paused, then brushed a loose strand of hair out of her eyes. "Your father sure knows how to play out a story, doesn't he?"

"Sure does," Jimmy said. "I mean, a giant frozen woodchuck? Come on!"

His mother laughed. "I know," she said. "He has a wild imagination."

"Yeah," Jimmy said. "Sure does."

He fiddled with the doorknob to his parents' bedroom. "But you don't think he really . . . ?"

"Went to the police?" his mother said. She shook her

head. "No, he probably just stepped out to get some fresh air."

Jimmy wanted to believe it. After all, a father who made up wacky stories was cool. But a father who *believed* those stories—well, that was something else altogether. His mom seemed worried.

"Now give me a hug," she said. "A big one."

Moments later Jimmy was slipping quietly past Imogene, headed for bed. By the time he fell asleep, he had put aside all doubts of his father's sanity and was looking forward to joking with him the next morning. "Hey, Dad," he'd say, "meet any frozen quadrupeds on the way home last night?" And his father would smile, rub a large hand through his hair, and say, "You like that one? Think it'll be a good story?" And Jimmy would nod. "Great," he'd say. "Go for it."

Who knew? Maybe *The Attack of the Frozen Woodchucks* would become his father's first published work.

With that thought, Jimmy rolled over and fell asleep.

TWO

"And How Long Were Those Whiskers, Ma'am?"

MOST MORNINGS JIMMY WOKE TO THE SOUND OF Imogene wandering into the living room, loudly demanding a sippy cup. But the next morning the doorbell woke him, followed by the sound of footsteps and muffled voices. By the time Jimmy roused himself, Imogene had already turned on *Sesame Street* and placed Jimmy's broken Game Boy on her lap for more "fixing." Jimmy's mother was standing in the hall, still in her nightgown, talking to two police officers.

"So let me get this straight," the first officer was saying. According to a badge on his uniform, his name was Lowe. He was a squat, fat man in such bad shape that Jimmy wondered how he could chase a jaywalking grandmother, let alone a real criminal. "Your husband went to bed next to you last night. This morning he was gone."

11

"That's right," his mother said. "Without a trace."

"Mom?" Jimmy asked. "What's going on?"

She turned to him with wide, tearful eyes. "He came home last night. But this morning . . ."

Her voice trailed off.

"Maybe he's staying at a friend's, ma'am," the second officer said. Her badge read GARCIA.

Where Officer Lowe appeared too old and chubby for the job, Garcia seemed too young.

Jimmy's mother shook her head. "Oh, no. I don't think so. He would have told me."

"You're sure?" Officer Garcia went on. "Because most missing persons just forget to say where they're going."

"Maybe he went to write at work?" Jimmy said.

He imagined his father bursting through the door, waving the first pages of *The Attack of the Frozen Woodchucks*. But his mother shook her head again.

"I already called the office."

"He doesn't always answer there," Jimmy said.

"I had the weekend receptionist check his desk and the library."

Jimmy still wasn't worried. His father had to be *somewhere*. Getting milk. Taking a walk. Writing at the local

Greek diner. People didn't just disappear out of their beds in the middle of the night. Officer Lowe didn't seem particularly concerned either. He took a croissant out of a paper bag and helped himself to a big bite, scattering crumbs onto the carpet.

"Okay," he wheezed between chews. "Is there anything else you can think of that might help us track him down? Anything unusual?"

Jimmy's mother looked at her hands, as if deciding whether or not to continue. In the background, Big Bird was saying, "Today's letter is G!"

"Mom?" Jimmy said.

"Well," she said. "There was something."

"Ma'am?"

"Grape begins with G!" Big Bird announced. "So does gorilla!"

His mother shot Jimmy a miserable glance, then looked to the two officers.

"There was a whisker."

Earlier that year, during a dodgeball game, Jimmy had run headfirst into Clyde Hamilton, the biggest boy in his grade, and had the wind knocked clear out of him. That's how he felt now.

"A whisker?" he squeaked.

Was his father's disappearance the work of a giant woodchuck?

"And something furry brushed against my leg. At least I think it did. I was half asleep."

Out of the corner of his eye, Jimmy saw the two cops doing their best not to smile. Officer Lowe shoved the rest of the croissant into his mouth, then washed it down with a swig of coffee.

"Do you have a cat, ma'am?"

His mother shook her head.

"Maybe it was a squirrel," Officer Lowe said. "Or a rat." He smiled and wiped his mouth with his sleeve. "I saw one the other day as big as my mother's St. Bernard."

"No," Jimmy's mom said. "I'm certain this wasn't a rat."

Garcia cleared her throat. "If it wasn't a cat or a rat, where do you think this whisker came from?"

Jimmy could tell that his mother was forcing herself to remain calm. But she was spared having to answer. Imogene tossed Jimmy's Game Boy aside and shouted from the couch.

"Giant frozen woodchuck, dummies!"

The officers looked at Imogene, then at each other.

Jimmy could only imagine what they were thinking. They had walked into a family of lunatics.

"A giant woodchuck, eh?" Lowe said. "Who's that? One of Big Bird's friends?"

Imogene wasn't amused.

"No!" she said, hands on hips. "The one I see with Daddy!" She pointed in the general direction of the park. "You go get him! Go! Go!"

With that, she turned back to the television and began to suck her thumb. *Elmo's World* had just begun.

Officer Lowe smiled almost to himself. "Frozen woodchuck, eh? Well, who wouldn't be frozen with the winter we've had?"

He chuckled at his own joke, belly jiggling, leaving Garcia to take control of the investigation.

"So, Mrs. Weathers? You saw this whisker and then what?"

Jimmy's mother began to pace the small living room. "It was all such a blur. Like I said, I was half asleep. But I did hear a rustling in the sheets. I thought Richard was just getting up to use the bathroom or to get a drink. But then I felt the whisker tickle my leg." She paused. "And then I saw—" She broke off.

"Who?" Lowe said. "You saw who?"

Jimmy's mother sighed. "I saw two front teeth."

Though it was warm in the apartment, Jimmy felt a sharp chill.

"Front teeth, ma'am?" Garcia asked.

"Yes." She paused. "Buckteeth."

Jimmy shuddered.

"Woodchuck," Imogene shouted over the theme song to *Elmo's World*. She pointed wildly toward the window. "In park! You go!"

Moments later, with promises to follow up on any leads, the officers were gone. But Jimmy knew that the last place they were going was Central Park to investigate a woodchuck. Most likely they were headed straight to the precinct to have some more coffee and make jokes. And Jimmy had to admit that if *he* were a cop in the station, he would laugh along with everyone else. After all, the whole thing was ridiculous. People just weren't kidnapped by thirty-foot rodents. Wasn't it more likely that his father was simply out for a walk and his mom had seen things in her sleep? Maybe the tickle of that giant whisker was his father running his hand over her leg, saying good-bye? But what about the two buckteeth?

The more Jimmy thought it through, the more he felt that Imogene was right. Crazy as it sounded, the only explanation was that last night the giant woodchuck, very much unfrozen, had moved silently but swiftly out of the park, reached a humongous paw through the open window of Jimmy's parents' bedroom, and whisked his father away. Worse, it was clear that dadnapping by woodchuck was not a crime that the New York City police department took seriously. Which meant one thing. Jimmy drew in a deep breath, steeling himself for the challenge ahead: His father's rescue was up to him.

THREE

Pods and Pawprints

JIMMY ALWAYS LOOKED FORWARD TO SUNDAY afternoons at his mother's tea shop, when the neighborhood writers would read, dancers would dance, and inventors would show off their latest inventions as the customers enjoyed their drinks and pastries. The entire Weathers family had participated at one time or another. Numerous times his father had read from his children's books. Once Jimmy and his mom had played the bongos while Imogene shared a short poem she called "Love Song to Potty."

Jimmy had been looking forward to that afternoon's event. A local performance artist named Captain Dan was set to recite the poetry of Walt Whitman while riding a unicycle and juggling four volleyballs. Obviously, in light of the terrible events of the evening before, Captain Dan was canceled. Moments after the police left, Jimmy's mom called an old friend from college who worked as a private detective and talked her way into an appointment.

"I'm closing the shop today," she told Jimmy after getting dressed. "You'll have to watch Imogene. Just don't let her sit in front of the TV all morning."

With *Elmo's World* over, Imogene had pressed play on the DVD player, turning on *Mary Poppins*. Jimmy could hear his sister singing along with Julie Andrews to "A Spoonful of Sugar."

"Don't worry," he said. "I won't."

Emma gave Imogene a quick kiss and was out the door. The minute his mother left, Jimmy made a phone call of his own. Let his mom consult with a private eye. Jimmy didn't need professional help to know where to start the investigation. Perhaps William H. Taft the Fifth wasn't a detective, but he *was* the great-great-great-great-nephew of William H. Taft, the fattest man ever to serve as president of the United States. He was also Jimmy's best friend.

"Hey!" Jimmy said when his friend came to the phone, then quickly brought him up to date on the events of the previous hours.

"Usual place," William answered. "Half an hour."

Jimmy underestimated the time he would need to get

out of the house with a two-and-a-half-year-old. By the time he managed to pull Imogene away from *Mary Poppins* and get her dressed, he was running fifteen minutes late. Then, with one foot out the door, Imogene had insisted on taking a bag of Cheerios, a pair of sunglasses, a copy of *One Fish, Two Fish, Red Fish, Blue Fish*, and Jimmy's broken Game Boy in her purple backpack. Finally leaving his apartment building, Jimmy turned down 100th Street, pushing Imogene in her stroller in front of him.

"Wait!" Imogene cried after a few steps.

Jimmy knew what was coming next. Imogene reached to her side and pressed a button. The small motor under her stroller turned over and began to rumble, kicking up dirt.

"Now push!" Imogene said.

Jimmy grabbed the stroller handlebars and began to jog down the street. Since the sidewalk sloped slightly downhill, it was hard to tell if the motor was helping them along or not. But Imogene seemed to think so.

"I go!" she shouted. "Go!"

A half block down, Jimmy saw the familiar sign for Emma's Tea on the corner of Columbus. William was seated at one of four small round tables outside the shop, writing vigorously in a spiral binder. Before him was a book, bent at the middle and dog-eared. Next to the book was a bag from City Donuts. Considering how much William ate, it was no surprise that he was chubby, especially given that his great-great-great-great-uncle was so large, he had once gotten stuck in the White House bathtub.

"Yo!" Jimmy called.

Continuing to scribble, William did not look up. Jimmy brought the stroller to a stop, clicked off Imogene's motor, then leaned into his friend's ear.

"Yo!"

Still writing with his right hand, William held up an open palm with his left. Without missing a beat, Imogene slapped it.

"Yo! Yo!" she said. "Yo! Yo! Yo!"

Only as Jimmy moved to release Imogene's stroller straps did William finally look up.

"Frozen woodchucks, huh?"

Jimmy nodded. He knew that William would take the news at face value, no questions asked. He was that kind of friend.

"Just one. And big, too."

William whistled. Then he smiled.

"What?" Jimmy asked.

"You know me." William nodded at his binder. There

were pages covered with notes, arrows, and mechanical drawings. "Just thinking how my turbo-powered portable rocket engine can help."

Jimmy grinned. Even though his uncle had been a president, William's passion was outer space, not politics. In third grade he had spent a full year on a design for a telescope made primarily of discarded contact lenses (his father was an optometrist) that would allow the viewer (or so William had claimed) to locate an undiscovered strain of poison ivy on the third moon of Jupiter. All Jimmy saw when he looked through his friend's telescope was a neon sign reading HOTEL/CHEAP RATES flashing atop a nearby building.

In fourth grade William had devoted hours to transforming a purple go-cart into a rocket ship designed to carry him and a group of select passengers to Anthador, a nearly invisible planet between Venus and Mercury. Once there he planned to rechristen it "Taftia" and, like his uncle, serve as president. "I'm not much of a leader on Earth," he had told Jimmy. "Maybe I'll do better on my own planet."

But when his go-cart hadn't made it more than five feet off the ground, let alone out of Earth's atmosphere, William had lowered his sights. Fifth grade had been devoted to the construction of a rocket engine that could fit into any New York City yellow cab. "I don't know about you," said William, "but I like to get across town in a *hurry*."

"Well, this might be your chance to use it," Jimmy said. "If my dad was really taken by a giant woodchuck, we might need a whole fleet of rocket-powered cabs to get him back."

William laughed and flipped his shaggy brown hair out of his eyes. "You know, before my uncle was president, he was secretary of defense. I bet he would have thrown my new engine on the backs of all the horses in the cavalry!" William sighed and looked wistfully out on 100th Street. "We might have won World War I in a week."

Jimmy was very used to nodding politely whenever his friend went off about his uncle. He didn't have the heart to mention that by the time World War I was fought, William H. Taft the first was no longer president and American troops were already beginning to use tanks.

"Yeah," Jimmy said. "That's a bummer."

"Big time," William said. Then the large boy shook off the pain of a missed opportunity and turned back to the issue at hand. "Question: You don't think your parents are playing some weird prank, do you?"

Jimmy shook his head. "My mom was pretty upset. And she's not the type who would lie to the police."

"And she's certain that she saw the whisker and buckteeth?"

"She's certain, all right."

William closed his binder and stuck his ballpoint

behind his ear. "So where do we begin?"

As the two boys talked, Imogene had taken a bite of William's doughnut, then plopped herself back in her stroller and occupied herself by leafing through *One Fish, Two Fish, Red Fish, Blue Fish*. Now she stood back up.

"Go to woodchuck!"

The two boys exchanged a glance, then laughed.

"Imogene's been a step ahead of everyone on this from the beginning," Jimmy said.

"Go to woodchuck," William repeated. "Hard to argue with that."

Imogene beamed, then glanced at William's doughnut. "More?"

MOMENTS LATER JIMMY WAS PUSHING IMOGENE INTO Central Park at 103rd Street, with William at his side. After the brief thaw, another cold front was hitting the city. With a growing chill in the air, only a few parents and well-bundled children were using the playground. The sun was hidden behind a darkening cloud.

"Okay, Genie," Jimmy said, releasing his sister's shoulder straps. "Where were you and Daddy playing when you saw the squirrel that led you to the giant woodchuck?"

Imogene jumped out of the stroller. Once she was standing, she took stock of her surroundings. She then pointed to a clearing down a short hill.

"We play there!"

"Okay," William said. "Let's cruise."

"Wait!" Imogene called.

Jimmy turned. "What?"

She tugged at her brother's sleeve. "Carry me?"

Jimmy sighed. When she was a baby, carrying his sister was no big deal. Now she was thirty pounds.

"Can't you walk or sit in your stroller?"

Imogene shook her head. "No walk. No stroller."

As William pushed the empty stroller, Jimmy scooped his sister into his arms and walked down a short hill. The clearing was set off about thirty feet from a concrete path and surrounded on three sides by tall trees. The grass was still wet with recently melted snow.

"Is this where you were?" Jimmy asked.

Imogene nodded.

"Where did the squirrel go?" William asked.

Without missing a beat, Imogene pointed to a narrow space between two tall oaks.

"Through there?" Jimmy asked.

"You go." Then without missing a beat, she began to

sing. "Doe, a deer, a female deer!"

While Jimmy carried his singing sister, William lugged the stroller. Jimmy soon wondered if he was crazy to follow the directions of a toddler. The woods were thicker than he had imagined. With every step, drops shook off the trees onto his hat and jacket. After ten steps he stopped. In the middle of the woods now, Jimmy found it almost possible to imagine that he wasn't in New York City at all.

"This is sort of creepy," William said, coming up behind. Without a hat, his hair was slicked back with water. His chubby cheeks were red. "Are you sure this is right?"

Again Imogene didn't hesitate. She stopped singing and pointed them deeper into the woods.

"Go!"

Jimmy and William exchanged a glance. Jimmy shrugged, shifted Imogene's weight to his other arm, and moved forward. The trees grew closer together. A wet branch hit Jimmy in the face. He fell to his knees.

"Genie," he said. "Are you sure . . . ?"

Before he could finish the sentence, he saw an opening in the tree line. In a few more steps they stood at the edge of a clearing.

"I see egg!" Imogene cried, and struggled out of her brother's arms.

Then he saw it: the pod, cracked into pieces.

Jimmy thought it did resemble the dinosaur eggs on display at the natural history museum. Moments later the three children were gathered around the pod. Jimmy rubbed a palm over the surface of the nearest part. It was smooth, like the inside of a seashell.

"Woodchuck grow here," Imogene said.

William looked to Jimmy. "You really think that's what it was? A woodchuck pod?

Jimmy shrugged. "What else could it be? An old fossil?"

"Maybe a papier-mâché project for school," William said. "Some kids might've dumped it here. You know, when he was president, my uncle—"

This time Jimmy didn't let his friend finish the thought.

"I don't know," Jimmy said. He rubbed the pod again. "This doesn't feel like papier-mâché to me."

He took a step back to get a better view. But his foot dropped farther than he had expected, and he fell backward. Righting himself, Jimmy gasped. He was standing in a giant footprint.

"Oh, my God!" William called. "There's another!"

The second was four feet or so from the first. Then Jimmy spotted a final print by the edge of the clearing. Just beyond, in the woods, two trees had been knocked down.

Obviously some large animal had pushed its way out.

"Holy mother of the Federal Reserve!" William exclaimed.

"One hundred percent weird," Jimmy said.

Imogene was in no mood to reflect on the strangeness of the world. After jumping in and then out of the first footprint, she pulled impatiently on Jimmy's coat.

"We find woodchuck," she said. "Move!"

FOUR

At the Precinct

BEFORE THEY COULD STOP HER, IMOGENE WAS following the path of the footprints back into the woods, shouting, "Go! Go!" Soon the woods met a field where Jimmy, William, and Imogene, now back in her stroller, followed the footprint path to the drive that circled the park.

"Bummer," William said. "Lost him."

"Maybe not," Jimmy said, and ran across the street to see if he could pick up the trail on the other side. Moments later he was back.

"Any luck?" William asked.

Jimmy shook his head. "Nothing. He must've traveled on cement from here."

"What next?" William asked.

Jimmy thought it over. "Well, we have the proof, right? The pod and the footprints."

"Yeah?"

"So maybe the police will take it more seriously now." He looked to Imogene. "Sound good, Genie? We'll show the police the pod."

To Jimmy's surprise, Imogene greeted that news with less enthusiasm than he had expected. Instead, she yawned.

"Lean back," she said.

Time for her morning nap. Jimmy adjusted the stroller seat so it reclined. As Jimmy pushed her back to Central Park West, Imogene put on her sunglasses and stuck her thumb in her mouth. By the time they reached the police station at 100th Street, she was fast asleep. William helped Jimmy carry the stroller up the short flight of stairs into the station. Though there was no one ahead of them, the two boys had to wait five minutes for the desk sergeant— his badge read PEARCE. He was sorting out information that had to do with a traffic ticket. When he was finally done, he looked up.

"What can I do for you boys?"

Jimmy's heart began to pound. Until that morning he had never actually spoken to a policeman. On top of that, a dark five-o'clock shadow made Pearce look more like a crook than a cop.

"Boys?" the sergeant repeated. "Is there a problem?"

Jimmy looked to William, hoping his friend would pick up the slack and explain the situation. But when William met Jimmy's glance by nervously looking at his feet, Jimmy knew it was up to him.

"It's about my father," he said.

"Lemme guess." Pearce smiled and rubbed his stubble. "He's making you take out the garbage and you don't like it?"

Jimmy forced a smile. "I wish it was that simple."

Pearce raised his eyebrows, then nodded at Imogene, still asleep with her thumb in her mouth. "He's making you take care of your kid sister?"

"No," Jimmy said. "I actually like that."

"Cute kid," the officer said.

"Most of the time," Jimmy said.

"Then what's up?"

"Well, it's going to sound weird."

"Trust me," Pearce said. "In this job, I'm used to it."

Jimmy paused. The obvious starting point was the night before, when his father and Imogene had come home talking about the amazing thing they had seen in the park. The question was how to describe it without the officer dismissing Jimmy as a crackpot. After a moment's thought, Jimmy decided that his best chance was to simply spit out the whole insane story as fast as he could. At least that way he would get the whole thing out without being stopped.

"Okay, then. If you're ready for weird," Jimmy began, "here's weird!"

Out it came, even faster than he had intended, a flurry of information. To Jimmy's amazement, Officer Pearce didn't crack a smile—not even once. Picking up even more speed as he went, Jimmy finished with the discovery of the broken pod and footprints.

"So will you send someone? We'll lead you right there."

For a moment Jimmy was convinced that Pearce would help—that behind his thick five-o'clock shadow was an officer with a heart of gold, a man who had devoted his life to helping the citizens of New York, no matter how absurd the problem . . . but then the moment was gone. Jimmy realized that he had drawn a small crowd of interested and amused cops, all exchanging smiles. Worse, Officer Lowe was in the center of the group, this time munching on a bagel smeared with scallion cream cheese.

"Told you guys," he said. "I could never make up something as good as a frozen woodchuck."

As laughter filled the small room, Jimmy's heart sank. Just as he had thought—his father's case had become the station joke. But perhaps he hadn't misjudged Officer Pearce after all.

"Okay, guys," he said to the other policemen. "Enough already." That was all it took for the officers to go their separate ways, perfectly happy to leave the problem of a couple of crazy kids to someone else. Then Pearce leaned back in his chair and stroked his chin.

"Your father?" he said. "Is he around six feet tall and thin?"

Jimmy felt his heart jump. He and William exchanged a glance.

"Why?" Jimmy said. "Have you seen him?"

Without answering, Pearce riffled through some papers, then shook his head and turned to another pile.

"Last night," he said, finally pulling out a yellow report. "At ten seventeen one Richard Weathers reported the presence of a pod in Central Park and an enormous woodchuck loose in the city."

The night before Jimmy had hoped that his father wouldn't report the woodchuck. Now he was thrilled that he had.

"So you saw him?" Jimmy said.

"Not me," Pearce said. "This is from the night shift."

"What happened?" Jimmy asked. "Did a squad check it out?"

Pearce sighed. "I probably shouldn't be telling you this."

His voice trailed off.

"What?" Jimmy asked.

"There's more. You see, last night at two we picked up a homeless guy. He was hysterical. Really upset. Brought him in the station to figure out what was going on. Turns out he saw something."

"Saw what?" William said.

"A monster, he called it." Pearce paused. "Then he saw a flying saucer take off from a field near 106th Street. Said it was a real mother of a ship."

Jimmy felt like he had been kicked in the head. Did this mean that his father been transported to outer space?

"Where is this guy?" Jimmy said. "I've got to talk to him."

"That's gonna be tough."

"Why?" William asked.

"You heard of Bellevue?"

Jimmy's heart sank. Every city kid knew about Bellevue—a psychiatric hospital.

"The guy was a little bit crazy and also drunk," Pearce said. He waved a hand. "I probably shouldn't have even told you."

"But you'll send a squad to the park now?" Jimmy asked. "To look at the cracked pod?"

Pearce paused. Jimmy could tell what was coming

next—the easy letdown. "Sorry," he'd say. "Too much street crime. We just don't have the manpower." Jimmy suddenly felt himself become brave.

"Please!" he said. "My dad is missing! Gone! Possibly lifted into outer space! You've got to help us!"

For a moment Jimmy thought Officer Pearce would drag him by the ear and toss him onto the street. Either that or finally laugh. But instead he shook his head.

"She's gonna kill me," he muttered, then reached for the phone. "Yeah. Hello. Get me Garcia. Okay. Right."

He placed the phone back on the cradle and winked.

"Wow," Jimmy said. "Thanks!"

"She'll be right out. Find you your woodchuck."

With that Pearce turned back to his papers. The boys pushed Imogene's stroller to a row of benches and sat down.

"Man oh man," William said. "You really handled that guy."

Jimmy shrugged. "You'd do the same thing if it was your dad."

Just then Imogene stirred. Jimmy jumped to his feet and walked the stroller up and down the waiting room until she settled back to sleep. As he was sitting again, he saw Officer Garcia, wiping her mouth with a napkin and holding a bag of chips. Apparently Pearce had interrupted an early lunch break.

"Thanks for coming out," Jimmy said.

"I hear you boys have some leads."

She was polite but all business. Jimmy knew he had only a minute or two to convince her to come back to the park.

"We have something for you to see," he said. "A clearing in the park with a pod. And there are giant footprints leading into the fields."

Garcia nodded, then sat on the bench next to Jimmy.

"A pod and footprints, huh?"

"That's right," Jimmy said. "Can we take you there?"

To Jimmy's dismay, Officer Garcia didn't move toward the door. Instead she put another chip in her mouth, considering what to say next.

"Listen," she said finally. "I know your dad is missing. I know that must be very upsetting."

"But . . ." Jimmy began.

"But you've got to know we're doing everything we can," Garcia went on. "We sent out an all-city bulletin on your father. This morning Officer Lowe and I interviewed people in the neighborhood, asking if they had seen him. Don't worry. We're on the case. We'll get him back."

Jimmy prided himself on being honest. He never lied

to his parents and never cheated in school. *Almost* never, anyway. But with his father's life on the line and Officer Garcia two seconds away from returning to her lunch, what else could he do? Though he hadn't been in a single school play in his entire life, and had never had any special interest in acting, Jimmy buried his head in his hands. Then he pretended to cry. He knew the sound of it well enough—he shared a room with a two-and-a-half-year-old. But then something strange happened. The fake tears became real. This wasn't a game. His father really *was* missing. The father he loved. The only one he had.

"Hey," Officer Garcia said gently. "It's all right."

It had been so long since Jimmy had really cried that he had forgotten how hard it could be to turn off tears once they began. William handed him one of Imogene's wipes. Jimmy blew his nose.

"Feel better?" Garcia asked.

Jimmy nodded.

"Please know that we're doing everything we can."

Jimmy looked up. He didn't care if his eyes were streaked red or if snot was bubbling out of his nose. This was his chance to make a final plea.

"Just come with us to the park," he said. "Please. Just

look. If you don't believe us then, I'll leave you alone. Promise."

Garcia looked over her shoulder to Pearce. On the phone with another call, he put his hand over the receiver.

"I'll cover for you," he said.

Jimmy's spirits brightened. Garcia had no choice now—she had to go! But suddenly Officer Lowe was moving into the room. To Jimmy's surprise, he was jogging!

"We've got a robbery," he said. "Let's go!"

Garcia turned quickly to the boys.

"Sorry," she said, but Jimmy could tell that she was relieved. "I'll be in touch about your dad."

Without another word, she ran for the door.

Test Flight

THAT AFTERNOON, JIMMY STOOD ON THE ROOF OF William's building. With the day getting colder, a light snow was dusting the city. But if William felt the cold, he didn't show it. On his hands and knees, he was tinkering with a purple go-cart that he had rigged for flight. His black binder was open at his feet to a page of scribbles, arrows, and rough mechanical drawings.

"You really think this'll fly?" Jimmy asked.

He looked over his friend's contraption doubtfully. A giant glass top, now open, folded down over the driver and two passenger seats. An enormous engine was perched on the back. On top of the motor itself an intertwining series of metal tubes twisted five feet into the air. Idling at a low speed, the engine belched a light plume of green smoke.

William rubbed his hands together excitedly. "Don't worry," he said. "We'll get airborne. I can't believe I didn't think of this before. You remember the rocket I designed last year?"

"You mean the one that crashed into the lamppost and caught on fire?"

William waved a hand. "That won't happen again. Look at this new engine!"

"I'm looking," Jimmy said. "But isn't this the engine you made to fit inside a yellow cab?"

"That's why I'm making adjustments!" William said, irritated. He looked to his binder, then nodded toward a large toolbox on the ground near Jimmy. "Just pass me the wrench, okay?"

Jimmy sighed and looked through the box. There was an eggbeater, a two-headed hammer, and a pair of scissors that collapsed into a screwdriver. It took Jimmy a moment, but he finally found a wrench and handed it over. William twisted two screws on the side of the cart, then reached up and took a good whack at one of the metal tubes that rose above it. Instantly the light green smoke coming out of the engine turned silvery orange. Then the engine backfired with a loud bang. Jimmy jumped.

"What's going on?"

"No worries," William said cheerfully. "All to be expected."

Jimmy was skeptical. After all, at NASA the most brilliant scientists in the world hadn't been able to send a man farther than the moon. What were the odds that his best friend's go-cart would work well enough to take them on an open-ended trip across the galaxy to find his father?

Then again, what other options did he have? As crazy as it seemed, Jimmy was now convinced that his father was being held hostage somewhere in outer space. The final proof had come after their disappointing visit to the police station. After Officer Garcia had refused to go and see the pod and footprints, Jimmy and William had pushed Imogene to the field at 106th Street, where Officer Pearce had told them the homeless man had reported seeing the spaceship take off. Upon arrival, the boys hadn't seen evidence of a flying saucer or Jimmy's father. But then they looked up. The upper leaves and branches of the trees circling the field had been badly singed.

"From the ship's afterburners," William said. He looked at Jimmy. "No doubt about it, dude. Your dad's in orbit."

Jimmy still wasn't convinced—not entirely. Weren't there other things that could have burned those treetops? Lightning? A low-flying plane? But then Imogene spotted it—the piece of evidence that absolutely linked his father to the spaceship.

"Daddy's story!" Imogene cried.

It was true! Caught in the singed branches of an oak was a piece of his father's favorite yellow writing paper. Jimmy climbed the tree in record time. Even before he got close enough to touch the paper itself, he recognized his dad's wild, curly scrawl.

"He must have fallen asleep holding his writing pad," Jimmy said as he put the paper in his pocket, vowing to return it to his father the minute he was rescued.

Which is when William first suggested that they try out his go-cart. But Jimmy wasn't ready—not yet. First he wanted to report back to his mother. Maybe she had come up with some leads of her own?

At home Emma admitted that her detective friend had turned down the case. "Imagine!" she said. "He told me I was crazy!"

After lunch Emma decided to take the boys' evidence to the police station to see if she would have better luck convincing them to take Richard's disappearance more seriously.

"I want to give them one last chance to do their job!"

She bundled up Imogene (by that point, it had started to snow) and returned to the precinct. The minute she was gone, William spoke up.

"No offense, but your mom is wasting her time. My rocket's our only chance."

This time Jimmy didn't argue. Unless the current crop of New York City police cars came equipped with wings, how else would he get to space to find his dad?

Now, as William tinkered with his engine, Jimmy looked off the roof of the building to the streets below. The snow was sticking. The wind was really beginning to blow. He zipped his coat up to the very top. It wasn't an ideal day for flying a plane out of an airport, let alone a homemade go-cart off a roof.

"There we go!" William called.

Jimmy turned. His friend's face was smeared with grease. He was holding the two-headed hammer. Somehow the smoke coming out of the go-cart was now light blue.

"You ready?" William said.

"You sure this thing will fly? Really sure?"

William pointed to the twisted mass of pipes rising above the engine. "See these pipes? Looks like a mess to you, right?"

Jimmy nodded.

"But it's this collection of pipes that gives the rocket the power to blast through the atmosphere." William waved his binder at Jimmy. "It's all here. It has to do with the theory of supercombustion dynamics."

Jimmy held up his hand. He knew from years of friendship that William would gladly explain every single page in his binder in intricate detail, peppered with odd information about his uncle, if he wasn't stopped immediately.

"It's all right," he said. "I believe you."

Jimmy looked at the flying go-cart. Though every fiber of his being was telling him to stay off it, what else could he do? With his father missing, he needed to get himself into outer space somehow. William did have talent—there was no question about it. "That boy may well found his own planet one day," Jimmy's father had once said. "He's a genius waiting for his moment!"

Maybe this was that moment? Jimmy had no choice but to roll the dice and hope.

William put a hand on Jimmy's shoulder. "I know that this whole thing could be interpreted as a little bit scary."

Jimmy forced a smile. "It wouldn't help my mom feel any better if I were dead."

William shook his head. "Not gonna happen. This ship is foolproof."

He handed Jimmy a silver bicycle helmet.

"A bike helmet?" Jimmy said.

"Yeah."

"That's going to protect me in a crash?"

William frowned. "There's not going to be any crash, all right? Now let's go! Hop in!"

Jimmy hesitated, then swung a leg high over the side of the cart and slid into the passenger seat nearest the window. To his surprise, it was snug and comfortable. William wedged himself in behind the steering wheel, adjusting his flight goggles.

"Okay," he said. "Strap in good and tight. Once this puppy gets going to three Gs, you might get tossed around a little."

This was sounding worse and worse by the second.

"Tossed around?" Jimmy said. He swallowed. "Say, William, shouldn't we test this thing first?"

"Test it?"

William was strapping himself in. To Jimmy's alarm, his seat belt was made out of an old leather belt.

"You know, with a dog or something?"

William looked offended. "How in the world would a Rottweiler or a poodle work the controls?" He frowned. "I thought you wanted to find your dad?"

"Of course I do," Jimmy said.

"So you saw that pod and those footprints and the burned trees in the park, right? He's in outer space, dude.

We have the proof. And the cops aren't going to do anything about it."

"Okay, but how are we going to find my father, once we're up there?"

William's eyes lit up. He reached inside his coat pocket and produced an old sweat sock.

"With this!"

"What?"

"It's your dad's!" William said. "I stole it from the laundry basket in the bathroom."

Jimmy frowned, then released his seat belt. "You're losing it."

"No, no!" William pushed him back into the seat. "Look!"

William pressed a purple button on the rearview mirror and a tray slid out of the dashboard. Without missing a beat, he dropped the sock into the tray. The tray closed with a bright *bing!*

"Meet my astral DNA directional scanner," he said cheerfully. "The machine reads your dad's DNA through his sock, then directs the ship to wherever he is in space. Cool, huh?"

Jimmy looked at his friend in complete disbelief.

William smiled. "Just relax." He winked. "I'm not the nephew of a president for nothing."

He flicked a large switch on the dashboard. With a loud whirr, the top lifted into the air.

"Watch your head!" William called.

Though he still harbored thoughts of escape, Jimmy looked up as the top dropped and enclosed them in the cockpit. William flicked another switch. Suddenly the control panel lit up in a dazzling array of lights. Jimmy was reminded of a Christmas tree, bulbs flashing.

"Wow," he said. "Cool."

William was all business now. His voice dropped a notch, his chin jutted out.

"Initiating flight protocol!"

Two more switches. Now the go-cart began to purr. Jimmy held on to the dashboard, his heart thumping like mad, as two wings slid out of the body of the cart. The engine started to belch plumes of yellow smoke.

"You ready?" William shouted.

Was it possible? Was this thing really going to work? William seemed to think so. Jimmy had never seen his friend so happy.

He nodded. "Ready!"

Even so, Jimmy realized he wasn't sure how the thing even took off. Did it go down a runway like a plane or lift off like a rocket? Before he had time to think it through,

William pushed the throttle. With a loud bang, the go-cart was off, spewing blue smoke.

"Hold on!" William called.

He cut the wheel. The go-cart swerved just in time to avoid a chimney. William slammed the throttle into overdrive. As the cart barreled across the roof, Jimmy gasped. The side of the building was rushing toward them! Then out of his side vision, Jimmy saw William pull the steering wheel toward him. To his amazement, he felt himself being pressed back in his seat and then lifted into the air. Just as suddenly, the roof of the building disappeared and the cart soared out over the white city streets!

"Stick this in your Department of Space Travel and Transportation!" the pilot cried. "William H. Taft the Fifth gets airborne!"

Jimmy looked down. The cars, stores, and people looked like they were pieces in his sister's dollhouse.

"Okay," William said. "Let's put this puppy in orbit."

He reached up and pressed a small black button. The go-cart instantly slowed and began to spin. Terrified, Jimmy gripped the sides of his seat so hard his hands turned white.

"Is this right?" Jimmy called over the noise.

William nodded. "Roger that."

He then began the short countdown. "Three, two, one!"

He pulled another lever on the ceiling. Looking out the side, Jimmy could see flames whoosh out of the afterburners.

"Blast off!" William cried.

Boom! The ship catapulted straight up, as though it had been shot out of a cannon. But just as suddenly as it rose, the ship stuttered in midair. The motor coughed. That was when Jimmy first noticed the smoke coming out of the engine. It was black.

"What's wrong?"

William was too busy flicking switches and pulling knobs to answer. The next thing Jimmy knew, the cart had stopped spinning. Its nose was pointing down. Jimmy was amazed at how quickly the people on the street began to grow in size. Cars, cabs, and buses came rushing into full focus. Through his terror, Jimmy saw that they were headed toward Broadway.

"Hold on!" William called.

Jimmy closed his eyes, expecting the worst. His poor mother! First her husband kidnapped by a giant woodchuck. Now her son smashed to bits in a homemade rocket! Incredibly, though, William remained calm under pressure. Yanking like mad on the steering wheel, he managed to get the nose of the ship pointing up. And just in time, too. With a loud screech, the back wheels hit pavement. When Jimmy opened his eyes, they were thundering down Broadway in heavy traffic, swerving wildly next to a bus. William stepped on the brakes. The cart slid sideways, shooting sparks, then righted itself. The wheels finally gripped the wet pavement, and William was able to regain control. A block later the cart screeched to a noisy halt. Breathless, Jimmy looked at his friend.

"That was close!"

William didn't seem upset. He flicked a few switches and nodded. "Takeoff was fine, but the retro-rocket was problematic." Then his face suddenly brightened. He had somehow maneuvered the cart to the front entrance of City Donuts. "Hey, want to grab something to eat?"

Jimmy blinked. "Eat?"

William nodded. "Flying always makes me hungry."

Eating his first doughnut (a chocolate glazed, his favorite), Jimmy was simply happy to be alive. But by doughnut number two, all thoughts had turned back to his father. He knew William well enough to know that his friend would want to haul his cart (now locked to a parking meter with three tickets on the windshield for speeding, possession of an illegal rocket engine, and reckless flying) back to his roof and try again. But Jimmy knew that the next crash landing might not be so smooth. No, they would have to find another way into outer space.

"Are you thinking what I am?" William asked.

He was also on doughnut number two. His preferred kind was Boston cream.

"That depends," Jimmy said. "Do you want to fix your go-cart and try again?"

"I'd love to," William said. "But we don't have the time."

Jimmy was surprised. He had expected William to fight for his machine.

"What then?" Jimmy asked.

William pushed his top front teeth out over his bottom lip as if they were horribly bucked. Jimmy blinked and put down his doughnut.

"You don't really think she can help us?"

William shrugged. "What other options are there?"

Jimmy knew the answer: none. For a moment they ate in silence.

"So how do we do it?" Jimmy asked finally. "Do we wander over to her house and say, 'Hi, Janice. Wanna fly us across the Milky Way?'"

William stuck the remaining half of doughnut number two in his mouth.

"Yeah," he said, mouth full. "Works for me."

SIX

Janice Claytooth

AFTER DOUGHNUTS, WILLIAM MANAGED TO GET THE go-cart working well enough to drive along the sidewalk to the back entrance of his building. But the elaborate array of pipes that sprouted from the engine made it impossible to fit inside the service elevator to take it back to the roof. Jimmy offered the back of his mother's shop as a temporary parking place.

"She'll be okay with that?" William asked.

Jimmy shrugged. "We'll move it tomorrow. Right now we've got to get going."

Another short ride through the city streets and the go-cart was parked and covered with a tarp in the back room of Emma's shop. After that the two boys walked fifteen blocks down Columbus Avenue. The temperature seemed to drop with each block. Traffic moved slowly through the fresh snow. Boys, girls, and parents dragged sleds toward the park. Everyone was bundled up.

A block from 85th Street, Jimmy sighed. "I still can't believe we're doing this."

Indeed, Janice Claytooth was the strangest kid in their class, an honor she had held since first grade. Her skin was as pale as a piece of white notebook paper and her teeth were wildly bucked. But even more striking than her looks was her manner. She almost never talked, and when she did, it was about one thing: flying saucers. She claimed to have one in her father's brownstone.

"This is pretty desperate," William admitted. "But you know what? Great leaders are often forced to make tough decisions."

Jimmy smiled. "Who's the great leader here? You or me?"

"Me, of course," William said. "It's in my blood."

The two boys turned up 85th Street toward the park and were soon chasing each other, tossing snowballs. Moments later they stopped in front of a brownstone. A short flight of steps led to a large, black door that looked as though it hadn't been cleaned in years. William leaned heavily on a small metal gate outside the house.

"It doesn't look like anyone's home," he said, winded from the short run.

Jimmy nodded. The building was five stories high and every single window was dark.

"We're sure this is the right place?" he asked.

William nodded. "Our class list said it was number six."

Tacked above a thin mail slot was a rusted 6. Due to a loose nail, the number had flipped almost completely upside down, giving it the appearance of a slightly off-kilter 9.

"One thing for certain," William went on. "Her dad has serious bucks."

Jimmy nodded. Every city kid knew that a five-story home near Central Park cost a fortune. Still, Jimmy found himself feeling sorry for Janice. In five years she hadn't ever played tag at recess or had a single playdate. Then he remembered something else.

"You heard about her mom?"

"Yeah," William said. "Fell into the seal pond at the Central Park Zoo when Janice was in kindergarten, right?"

Jimmy nodded. The story went that she had been pulled out by police, but had caught pneumonia and died. Again Jimmy gazed up and down the large brownstone. Who cared if Janice had five floors to kick around in? With no mom and no friends, it just seemed like more space to be lonely in.

"So?" William said. "Are we going up?"

Suddenly Jimmy was tempted to forget the whole

thing. Maybe—just maybe—his father was back in the apartment waiting for him. "Sorry for the trouble," he would say with a smile. "I was doing research on my next book at the natural history museum. Spent an entire day studying the migratory patterns of the water buffalo." It was a nice thought. But Jimmy knew it was just wishful thinking. His father was gone. Sad as it was, Janice Claytooth was their best hope.

"Come on," he said.

He opened the gate and jogged up the short flight of steps. Then he pressed the doorbell, a small gray button that used to be white. The boys waited. No answer. Jimmy pressed his ear to the door and listened.

"Not home," he said.

Despite what it meant about the possibility of finding his father, Jimmy was relieved. The house looked creepy.

"Give it one more try," William said.

As Jimmy raised his fist to knock, the door suddenly swung open. Jimmy blinked. Standing in the entryway was a better-dressed version of Janice in her early teens. The Janice Claytooth the boys knew from school wore frayed blue jeans and T-shirts. This older Janice was dressed for a day at the riding ring in a white blouse, blue breeches, and freshly shined boots. In her right hand was a riding crop.

Then the girl smiled, exposing a row of straight, beautiful teeth that lit up her face.

"Yes?" she said. "Can I help you?"

Jimmy felt suddenly nervous. He didn't meet many older girls, let alone pretty ones.

"Hi," he finally managed. "Is Janice home?"

The girl seemed confused. "Wait. You actually want to see Janice?"

"What's so weird about that?" William said. "Is she home?"

The girl laughed. "Home? She's always home! This is the first time Janice has had friends drop in since she was in pre-K. I should call *The New York Times*. This is news!"

Jimmy sighed. To go with her dead mother, Janice also had an obnoxious older sister. At least he thought the girl was her sister.

"Can we see her then?" Jimmy asked.

The girl still wouldn't give a straight answer.

"By the way, I know what you're thinking."

Jimmy wrinkled his brow. "You what?"

"I look like Janice only pretty, right? I've got a smile that could sink tugboats. She's got those hideous buckteeth. Admit it. You probably think I'm too good-looking to be related to her at all."

The boys were too embarrassed to answer; that was exactly what they had been thinking. The girl laughed.

"Knew it.... I'm Angelina," she said in a tone that said they should already know her name.

"Look," William said. "Can we see Janice?"

The girl shrugged and pushed the door open. Through the entryway was a foyer that led to a dining room and kitchen. "This way."

Moments later the boys were following her up a staircase that was so poorly lit and creaky that Jimmy half expected bats or a ghost to come flying down.

"So you guys are at Academy School?"

"That's right," Jimmy said.

Despite the fact that it was one of the hardest programs to get into in the city, Angelina was unimpressed.

"Public school is for losers," she said. "I wouldn't be caught dead in a dump like that."

"For your information," William said, "most of our nation's presidents have gone to public school. And our school is no dump."

By that point they were on the second floor, on the edge of what appeared to be a living room, sparsely furnished.

"Not a dump?" Angelina said. "I suppose you've heard of Rockland?"

Jimmy had. It was an elite private school on the East Side.

"Does Academy School give each student a new laptop?" the girl went on. "Do you have a brand-new Olympic-size swimming pool? Do you go horseback riding in Central Park for gym class?" She sighed. "Oh, whatever. Why am I wasting my breath? Janice is one flight up. Just follow the music."

With no good-bye, she jumped down the stairs three at a time.

"Man," William said. "What a jerk."

"Later," Jimmy said. "Listen." The sound of strings, winds, and timpani drifted down the stairway. "I never knew Janice liked classical music."

"We also didn't know she had an older sister," William replied. "But why would we? We've said three words to her in five years."

The boys followed the music up another flight, then down a hall lined with family pictures. Though there was an occasional photo of Janice, her face was almost always buried in a book. The few times she was looking at the camera, her mouth was shut tight in a vain effort to hide her buckteeth.

"Janice sure doesn't like having her picture taken," Jimmy said.

"Yeah," William said. "But her sister sure does."

It was true. For every one shot of Janice there were four of Angelina, running, jumping, always smiling, even in younger shots when she had braces. The last photo in the display showed Angelina atop a horse. Standing by her side was a short man, completely bald, who shared her same bright smile.

"Must be their dad," William said.

"But why no pictures of her mom?" Jimmy asked.

William shrugged. "If you ask me, this whole family is weird."

Jimmy nodded. "Come on."

The boys moved farther down the long hall. With each step the music grew louder, filling the air with rich violins, cellos, and woodwinds. At the end of the hall the words "GIRL GENIUS RESIDES WITHIN" were written across a pink door in jagged black paint.

"Shall we?" Jimmy asked.

"We're here, aren't we?"

Once again William waited for Jimmy to do the honors. Jimmy knocked twice, half hoping there would be no answer. No luck. Janice's voice rang out, louder through a closed door than he had ever heard it in school from a foot away.

"COME IN IF YOU WANT, BUT THAT'S NOT GOING TO STOP ME!"

Jimmy shot a glance at his friend, then pushed through the door.

After seeing the interior of the home, Jimmy expected Janice's room to be just as barren. Instead, it showed signs of life. Along with a bed, stereo, and TV, there were rows of bookshelves, filled with everything from girls' magazines to science books. Then Jimmy saw it. On her night table was a picture of a woman who looked exactly like Janice: same dark hair, same pale skin, and most important, same buckteeth.

Jimmy nudged William. "There's Mom."

William nodded, then looked at Janice. Dressed in her customary frayed jeans and T-shirt, she was seated behind a desk, typing on a laptop, sucking on a strand of hair, staring intently at her screen. Two lit candles stood on her desk, each making a small puddle of wax.

"My offer still stands," Janice said, still staring at her screen. "You can have my iPod and my flat-screen TV. The rest goes to the museum."

Jimmy and William looked at each other. Then William motioned toward Janice, who was still typing madly.

"Go ahead," he whispered.

"Uh, Janice?" Jimmy said. "It's us. Jimmy and William. You know. From school."

No response.

"Janice?"

Her head wheeled around as if on a pivot, staring straight ahead. Her buckteeth and pale skin made her resemble a surprised rabbit, up on its haunches in the middle of a road, trying to decide which way to run.

"Oh, I thought you were Narice, our cook."

"I'm sorry we didn't call," Jimmy said. His voice trailed off. He suddenly felt lousy about barging in. "Your sister let us in."

"Angelina?" Janice said. "Off to a pedicure, right? Or was she going to get her legs waxed?"

"No," Jimmy said. "A riding lesson, I think. Or does she always carry a whip?"

Janice clicked her computer mouse, stopping the music. The room was suddenly strangely silent.

"What was that piece anyway?" William asked. "It was nice."

Janice's eyes went wide. "Nice? Of course it's nice! It's Beethoven, idiot. Symphony number seven, second movement. What better music than a funeral march to inspire my suicide note."

"Your what?" Jimmy said.

"The trouble is," Janice continued calmly, "I can't figure out how I should do it. Should I boil myself in my daddy's hot tub? Or maybe it'd be better if I impale myself on one of the spears in the armor exhibit at the Met? Then again I could always climb Mount Everest and throw myself off the Hillary Step."

Jimmy and William looked at each other, stricken, then back at Janice.

"You're joking, right?" Jimmy said. "I mean, you aren't really going to boil yourself in your dad's hot tub, are you?"

"Well," Janice said, "that would be easier, though Mount Everest would be more exotic."

Janice's sad smile convinced Jimmy that she just might be telling the truth about her intention to end her life. He felt terrible about all the times he had made fun of her behind her back. In second grade he and two other guys had even stuck pencils in their mouths to look like buck-teeth, then hopped around her desk.

"Hey," Jimmy said. "Things can't be that bad, right? We can get you help. Can't we, William?"

William nodded. "Sure."

"Help?" Janice said. "I've already been to four psychia-trists. They can't do a thing. And you know why?" She was suddenly pacing. "I'm really not as unhappy as you think. I mean, I'm not the most well-adjusted kid in the city—I do have a dead mother, an obnoxious sister, and a distant dad—but there are kids worse off than me. No, what makes me want to end it all is something simple. Something that eats my soul to little nibbly bits." With that, Janice suddenly clenched her fists. Her face scrunched into a tiny ball. "NO ONE TAKES ME SERIOUSLY!"

Jimmy and William were stunned by Janice's sudden ferocious intensity. She threw herself on her bed and curled into a fetal position.

"You mean at school?" Jimmy asked.

He thought guiltily of all the times he had called her names like Rancid Screw-Loose.

"Yes, at school!" Janice yelled to her pillow. "And at home! Everywhere!" Just as suddenly as she had thrown herself on the bed, she sat up. "WHY IN THE WORLD WON'T ANYONE BELIEVE THAT I'VE CON-STRUCTED A SPACECRAFT CAPABLE OF TOURING THE GALAXY?"

Jimmy could see William trying not to smile. For his part, Jimmy felt a surge of hope, like a gust of cool air on a hot day.

"Wait, Janice," he said. "We believe you."

"Yeah," William said quickly. "Always have."

Janice narrowed her eyes. "Yeah, right. What about the time in second grade when you said, 'There goes Janice

Graygoof, the idiot who thinks she can fly'?"

William swallowed hard.

"Listen, Janice," Jimmy said. "Sometimes boys can say stupid things."

"Right," William said. "I didn't mean anything by it. The fact is—" William paused, then continued with no small amount of pride. "I build rockets, too."

Janice laughed. "Yeah. I've seen your designs."

William's eyes went wide. "You what?"

"That binder you carry around." She held out a hand. "Come on. Let's see!"

Janice's arm shot out. As quick as a frog nabbing a bug, she had it in her hands.

"Hey!" William said. "Private property!"

But Janice was already on her bed, flipping through the binder, smiling. Suddenly she stopped and read something more carefully. Then she laughed—not a little rabbitlike twitter, but a big, loud guffaw.

"What?" William said. "What?"

She held the binder to her nose and read out loud.

"'The Constitution of Planet Taftia! I, William H. Taft, the great-great-great-great-nephew of William H. Taft, the twenty-seventh president of the United States, do hereby declare that we the people of Taftia will let the chubby, slow kids choose teams at recess!'" She looked up. "Is it okay if I call you Mr. President from now on?"

"That's just a working draft!" William shouted. "Give it."

But Janice had already moved on. Glancing over her shoulder, Jimmy could see that she was skimming through a page of mathematical equations.

"I hope you aren't in a big hurry to found any planets," Janice said with a snort. "Your calculations are off. Way off!"

She tossed back the binder.

"What are you talking about?" William asked. "We flew a go-cart rocket just this afternoon."

"And I bet you got about two hundred feet into the air before crashing!"

Jimmy had never seen William look so hurt.

"What of it?" he snapped. "So I have to make a few adjustments."

"Sorry, Chubby," Janice said. "Your adjustments need adjustments."

"Listen," Jimmy said. "I know this is sudden. I know we've never really been friends." Moving back to her desk, Janice shot Jimmy a glance. "Okay, we haven't been friends at all. But here's the thing. Something's happened to my father. And we need your help."

Janice had turned back to her computer and was once

again typing. Jimmy could only assume that she was finishing her suicide note. As with Officer Pearce, he could tell that he had one shot to make his pitch. Even though her back was turned, Jimmy told Janice the story of his father's disappearance from the very beginning. When he was finished, he leaned against the window. For a moment the room was silent. Once again he felt like the world's biggest fool. Had he really just bared his soul to Janice Claytooth? A weirdo, lunatic girl who claimed to have a spaceship? It was all hopeless. Convinced that he would never see his father again, Jimmy felt about two seconds away from crying for the second time that day.

But then Janice spun slowly around in her chair. In the glow of her computer screen she made a strange sight. The candles glinted off her buckteeth.

"I was going to donate my spacecraft to the Museum of Science."

Against his better judgment, Jimmy felt hopeful. "Why do that," he said, "when you can help *us*?"

Janice peered closely at Jimmy, as if sizing up whether or not he was worth the trouble.

"Please," Jimmy said.

Just like that, Janice blew out the candles.

"Come on," she said, standing up.

"Where are we going?" William asked.

"Where are we going?" Janice said. "To my ship, that's where!" Then she smiled. "Bring your binder, Mr. President. You might learn something!"

SEVEN

The Fifth Floor

THE BOYS FOLLOWED JANICE UP THE STAIRS TO THE fourth floor. She led them across a large room, furnished by a lone, tattered sofa, then stopped by an iron door.

"My lab is up here," Janice said. "It's top secret. No one goes up. Not Angelina. Not Narice. Not anybody!"

"Not even your dad?" Jimmy asked.

He meant the question innocently enough, but clearly the mention of her father struck a chord. Janice scrunched her face up and scowled like she had just been force-fed an entire grapefruit.

"My dad?" she said. "He's not around much."

No wonder Janice and Angelina were so strange. They lived in a giant brownstone pretty much alone.

"What does he do, then?" William asked.

Jimmy was wondering the same thing. But now Janice's

scowl turned into a frown of outraged disbelief.

"You mean you don't know?" she said. Even in the dim light, Jimmy could tell she was deeply offended. "He invented the mute button!"

Jimmy wasn't sure that he had heard correctly. From the size of their home, he had assumed that Janice's dad was a high-priced lawyer or a banker. The last thing he expected was to find that he was an inventor, especially of something so strange.

"You mean like on remotes?"

"No, like on chickens," Janice snapped. "Of course on remotes."

"So that's why he's never home?" William asked. "He's working on new models?"

Janice rolled her eyes. After years of being the brunt of every joke in class, she was enjoying the chance to feel superior.

"Of course not," she said. "A mute button does only one thing. It makes a TV go quiet. Everyone knows that. But every time a remote is sold with a TV, VCR, or DVD player, my dad gets a few pennies. That's why we're so rich. Now he devotes himself to hobbies."

"Like what?" Jimmy asked.

"Different stuff," Janice said. "He sings with a Gilbert and Sullivan society. He collects corks from wine bottles. He has an outpost in Central Park where he traps polar bears. Lately he's been studying eighteenth-century hot-air balloons. Now come on! Do you want to see my spaceship or not?"

Jimmy nodded. "Sure."

Janice fumbled for her keys.

"Touchy, huh?" William whispered.

Jimmy nodded. But he could understand why. It was bad enough that her mom was dead, but what kind of dad preferred trapping nonexistent polar bears in Central Park to spending time with his own daughter?

"This way," Janice called.

The padlock released and she pushed open the door. Jimmy expected to walk directly into the lab. Instead, there was a spiral staircase that rose sharply into the darkness. Janice began to take the steps two at a time. In the half-light Jimmy gripped the banister and felt for the first step, then the second, doing his best to follow the sound of Janice's footsteps. As the staircase climbed higher and higher, Jimmy began to wonder if Janice wasn't enacting some elaborate plan to get revenge for all the insults she had received over the past five years. What if there wasn't a spaceship at all? What if Janice planned to hold him and William hostage in her attic? For a moment the fantasy seemed so real that Jimmy considered backing out.

Upstairs Janice flicked a switch, and bright light flooded the stairway. Looking up, Jimmy could see that the steps rose even higher than he had thought. The light at the top was so brilliant, he couldn't make out anything in the room. But he could hear Janice scurrying from one side of it to the other.

"What's she doing?" William whispered.

Jimmy held a hand up to his eyes.

"Getting ready, I guess."

The spiral staircase, the bright light, Janice's all-business attitude—they suddenly made Jimmy hopeful that Janice was the real deal—that if he continued up the steps, he really would step onto the bridge of a spaceship, complete with hundreds of different control panels, a captain's chair, and a full view of the galaxy; that in no more than a few seconds they would whoosh into space to rescue his dad. All of which made his disappointment even keener when he reached the top of the stairs. Instead of stepping into a spaceship, Jimmy found himself in a very ordinary attic. There was no picture window of the stars, no control panel with flashing lights. Instead, the room was old to the point of decay. One wall was lined with boxes filled with newspapers and magazines, another with broken household items and appliances. With a quick glance, Jimmy saw two rusted fans, an old refrigerator, a circular saw, and what appeared to be a giant stuffed guinea pig. Off to another side stood three green barber chairs.

Janice was rummaging through one of the large boxes when William came up from behind.

"She's a loon," he whispered.

Though he was thinking the same thing, Jimmy was too crushed to respond. But if Janice noticed Jimmy and William staring at her, she didn't let on. Moments later she pulled herself out of a storage bin holding three helmets and threw one to Jimmy and one to William.

"For you and you," she said.

Jimmy caught his.

"Listen, Janice," he began.

She turned. "What?"

"I mean, no offense, but—"

"What he's trying to say," William butted in, "is where is your ship?" He looked around, secretly happy to put Janice down the same way she just had him. "Don't tell me this is it?"

To Jimmy's surprise, Janice smiled.

"Novices," she muttered.

With that she turned to the wall and opened an old fuse box. She flicked an orange switch. As a soft whirring sound filled the room, Janice nodded to the ceiling.

"Take a look."

To Jimmy's surprise, the ceiling began to separate,

revealing a skylight. With another switch the skylight opened until Jimmy could feel wet snowflakes hit his face. Soon a soft mist filled the room and the floor began to vibrate. Then the wooden walls lifted, revealing shiny metal underneath. The flat ceiling began to curve down. Suddenly the room started to resemble the spacecraft of Jimmy's fantasies.

"Okay, guys," Janice said. "Have a seat."

She was standing at another fuse box now. With a flick of a large pink switch, the three green barber chairs slid noiselessly into the middle of the room.

"These?" Jimmy said.

"I had to make do with what I could find," Janice said. "Get on!"

It wasn't a request. Janice had completed a transformation from strange girl to starship commander. Now she was flicking more switches. A large dashboard, with buttons, knobs, and lights, rose up in front of Janice's barber chair. Two smaller dashboards rose up beside Jimmy's and William's. Then the wood floor separated, revealing a shiny new one underneath. At the same time, the ceiling finished curving inward and met the floor in the middle of the room. They were now entirely enclosed.

Jimmy was stunned. The musty attic had turned into a spaceship! The two boys got on their barber chairs and

strapped themselves in. By that point Janice was check-
ing the fuel gauge and making other last-minute prepa-
rations.

"Okay," she called. "*The Fifth Floor* is ready for flight."

"*The Fifth Floor*?" William asked. "That's its name?"

"Yup," Janice said. "And since I haven't flown her for
a few days, we'll get into space more quickly if you two
losers help me warm her up. You first, Mr. President. Give
a flick to the retro-rocket activator. That's the yellow switch
on your lower left panel."

Despite his irritation at Janice's nickname, William
looked at the panel on his dashboard. It took him a
moment, but he finally found the switch and flicked it. The
hum grew louder. Steam filled the room and then drifted
into the night sky. Very slowly Jimmy felt the ship begin to
rise like a hovercraft—up, up, up. Soon they were floating
a foot above the roof. Janice reached down and turned a
knob on the base of her barber chair. A steering wheel
dropped down from the ceiling directly in front of her.

"You next, Jimmy," Janice called. "Hit the light blue
button on your right."

Jimmy looked. His heart was racing. For a moment he
was confused. There were a hundred buttons to chose
from, and more than one was light blue.

"It's the one shaped like a kitten in the upper left corner," Janice said.

Jimmy found it. With a light whirr, the roof to the brownstone began to close beneath him.

"Good," Janice said.

She looked over her shoulder, grinning more broadly than Jimmy had ever seen. How could he blame her? If anyone deserved a chance to gloat, it was her.

"You guys ready?" she shouted.

Jimmy held on tight, trembling with terror and excitement. He knew it now for sure. This ship was going to work! But would they find his father?

"Ready!" he shouted.

"Floor it!" William cried.

Janice's hands were a flurry of motion on the controls. For a moment the ship sighed and seemed to lose power. Jimmy and William exchanged a glance. Could this be another dud? But then Janice slammed forward a large metal stick at the center of her control panel: the throttle. Jimmy felt the ship shake. Out of the corner of his eye he could see orange flames. Janice craned her neck and laughed.

"JANICE CLAYTOOTH WILL BE TAKEN SERIOUSLY!" she cried, and with a monumental boom *The Fifth Floor* shot into space.

EIGHT

Grindlepick

JIMMY WAS RATTLED, TOSSED, AND SHAKEN IN HIS SEAT. Just when he was certain that his chair was going to crash sideways onto the ship floor, he heard another boom. The glass screen at the front of the ship suddenly filled with stars, and Jimmy realized that they had left Earth's atmosphere. But there was more to come. As Janice continued to work the controls, an orange mist rose from the floor. The ship seemed to freeze in space, then began to buck up and down. For a split second the stars blurred. Then the screen went completely white, and with a giant whoosh the ship thundered even faster than before.

"What happened?" William asked.

Janice smiled. "This baby does light speed."

William's eyes went wide. "Light speed? How did you pull that off?"

Janice shrugged. "I was always good at math."

The ship seemed strangely still now, almost as if they weren't moving at all. The sky was illuminated by hundreds of bright stars. To the right, Jimmy saw the moon flash by. In the distance was a meteor shower. Janice was busy at the console.

"First stop is Grindlepick," she said.

"Grindlepick?" Jimmy asked.

Janice turned, excited. Now that they were on their way, she seemed thrilled that she was finally able to share her knowledge of outer space.

"It's where they grow all the galaxy's cotton candy."

William blinked. "You mean they grow cotton candy? Like in fields?"

"Exactly!" Janice said.

With that she turned back to the controls.

"This is too strange," William said.

A day earlier, Jimmy would have agreed. But given the events of the last twenty-four hours, a planet whose main industry was the production of cotton candy made perfect sense.

"Okay, guys," Janice said. "We're on automatic pilot. It's safe to get out of our seats now."

She released her seat belt. Stepping onto the floor, Jimmy was briefly worried that he would float to the ceiling. But Janice had rigged her ship to account for the loss of gravity. Awestruck, Jimmy looked out the window. For his part, William began to riffle through his binder. Moments later he looked up, face blank.

"I still don't get any of this."

Janice opened a compartment under the screen, pulled out a book, and tossed it across the room to William.

"Here," she said.

William read the title, *Light Speed and You*. He looked back up. "Who wrote this?"

"I self-published it last year," Janice said. "So far it's sold only one copy on Earth. But it's done pretty well in the rest of the solar system."

William sat back in his barber chair and opened the book as though it were a sacred artifact. At the same time, Janice joined Jimmy by the front screen. He was immediately struck by a change in her. For the first time he could remember, she was smiling.

"You like my ship?" she asked almost shyly.

Outside, a shooting star whipped by.

"Are you kidding?" Jimmy said. "It's amazing."

"It is pretty cool, huh?"

"So," Jimmy said. "This planet. Grindlepick. How far is it?"

Janice shrugged. "Oh, we should get there in"—she glanced over her shoulder to a digital clock on her console—"twenty-eight minutes."

Jimmy was stunned. He knew that it had taken the first Apollo rocket three days to reach the moon. And the unmanned Voyager expedition had taken years to reach Mars. As thrilled as he was to be in space, he had been worried that it would take years to find help.

"Do you think Grindlepick might be where the woodchuck is holding my dad?"

"Probably not," Janice said. "But I know some people there who might be able to give us information."

Information? It wasn't what Jimmy wanted to hear. He knew he was being carried millions of miles from Earth. His father could be anywhere—on a planet, a moon, even a star. The universe was enormous. What were the odds that a few people on a planet called Grindlepick would know what had happened to him?

"We'll find your dad," Janice said, picking up on his mood. "Just relax. We'll be there soon."

Jimmy got so engrossed looking at the stars, he almost couldn't believe it when Janice announced that they were close.

"Where is it?" he asked, searching the front screen.

Janice pointed. "There."

Jimmy squinted. Grindlepick looked no bigger than one of the stars. But soon the greens, reds, and blues of the planet's surface came into focus.

"Strap up," Janice said.

William had spent the entire trip in his chair trying to decipher the first few pages of Janice's book. He was so absorbed that Jimmy had to strap him in before jumping into his own seat.

It was then that Jimmy noticed the red blinking light above the screen.

"That's funny," Janice said.

"What is it?"

Janice flicked a switch. The red light now flashed blue.

"A distress signal from the planet's surface."

William looked up from Janice's book. "What's that mean?"

"Hard to say."

Jimmy immediately thought of his dad. What if the planet had been taken over by some new leader who passed laws saying that all earthlings were to be suffocated in barrels of cotton candy? What if his father had been the first victim?

"Do you think it's safe to land?" William asked.

But Janice was already focused on the controls. Now on

the outskirts of the Grindlepick atmosphere, the ship began to shake. Jimmy clutched the sides of the barber chair.

"Hold tight!" Janice called.

With a sonic boom they plunged into Grindlepick's atmosphere. Suddenly the ride smoothed out, and they were gliding through a light purple sky, past two orange moons. As Janice guided the ship down toward the planet's surface, Jimmy and William looked out the window over rows of pastureland. The fields were not green. Instead they were brighter colors—yellows, pinks, and oranges.

"Those are the cotton candy fields," Janice said. "They ship all over the galaxy."

Soon the ship was hovering over a lush yellow field. Janice gave the throttle a subtle push, and the ship began to descend to the planet's surface. Moments later they hit the ground with a soft bump.

"That's what I love about cotton candy," Janice said. "Easy landings. Okay, out we go."

"But wait," William said. During landing he had finally put down Janice's book. "What about the atmosphere? Will there be enough air to breathe?"

Janice smiled.

"What?" Jimmy asked.

Without saying another word, she pressed a button on

her console. A side door slid open, and a wonderful smell filled the ship. For a second the two boys and Janice sat and breathed deeply.

"It's like lemon," William said finally.

"Yeah," Jimmy said. "But I smell orange too."

"And strawberry, grape, cinnamon, chocolate, and lots of other good stuff," Janice said. "Come on outside. It's even better."

Jimmy unbuckled his strap and followed Janice and William outside the ship onto a soft field. He was surrounded on all sides by tufts of cotton candy, swaying five feet tall in a light breeze. While the smell was wonderful on the ship, outside it was overpowering. He suddenly felt ravenously hungry. It seemed like years since he had eaten those doughnuts.

"Wow," William said, looking hungrily over the fields. "Who would have thought cotton candy would grow so high?"

"It's almost time for the harvest," Janice explained. "Go ahead, pull some off. Take a bite."

The boys didn't have to be told twice. Together they walked to the edge of the field and reached up to a large yellow tuft. The cotton came off easily in their hands. When they put it in their mouths, it dissolved almost instantly, leaving a taste of lemon.

"It tastes different from back home," Jimmy said.

"That's because we earthlings like things sweet," Janice said. "The Grindlepick farmers add sugar to our shipments."

Jimmy and William took another bite.

"I like it better this way," William said.

Jimmy let the candy melt in his mouth while he gazed around him. Rows and rows of lush cotton candy bushes spread across rolling hills, swaying in a light breeze. In the far distance Jimmy saw what appeared to be pinto ponies grazing on tufts of orange cotton. Then he looked closer. Those animals weren't ponies at all—they were giant Dalmatians!

"Are those dogs?" he asked.

William was by his side. "They sure look it."

"Hey, Janice," Jimmy said.

But Janice was gazing over the beautiful landscape with a frown.

"That's funny," she said. "Someone usually comes out to meet me."

Which was when Jimmy remembered the distress signal. But before he could ask Janice what she thought was wrong, she muttered, "Oh, no," and stood on her tiptoes to get a better view—of what, Jimmy didn't know. Then, just like that, she broke into a flat-out run. Jimmy was stunned.

In all his years in recess, he'd never seen her so much as jog. At the edge of the first field she stopped and turned.

"Come on!" she shouted.

The next thing Jimmy knew, he was sprinting down a winding dirt path that cut through the heart of the yellow cotton candy field. Plants grew ten feet high, filling the air with an overpowering scent of lemon. But at that moment, Jimmy's entire focus was on trying to keep up with Janice. When the path curved, he lost sight of her altogether. A low-hanging plant brushed against his face—he tripped into the tufts and came up a second later with a mouthful of cotton candy.

"Since when is she so fast?" William asked, running up.

"Yeah," Jimmy said. He was almost too winded to talk. "Remind me to pick her first next time we're choosing sides in recess. Come on."

Jimmy led the way around the corner and down the path. As it curved up and back around, the color of the cotton candy changed from yellow to orange, then back to yellow. The boys ran into a grassy pasture. Janice was on her knees. From a distance, Jimmy thought she might be crying. He collapsed by her side.

"What's going on?" he asked.

Janice looked at him, eyes wide.

"What?" William asked, stumbling up from behind.

"The trees!"

"What trees?" Jimmy asked.

"That's the point!" Janice gestured to the field. "They're gone!"

When Jimmy looked again, he saw the pasture for what it really was: a field of gnarled tree stumps. And the stumps didn't look as though they had been cut neatly by a saw. Each one was riddled with tooth marks, gnawed straight to the ground.

And then Jimmy saw something even more chilling. Lying in a nearby field were rows and rows of cracked pods!

NINE

The Second Sighting

WILLIAM SAID IT FIRST.

"The woodchucks!"

Jimmy's thoughts turned instantly to his father. What if the giant rodents gnawed more than wood? What if his dad had been swallowed in a single gulp—a woodchuck appetizer?

"That sure explains the distress signal," Janice said.

She sounded worried. Jimmy shuddered, half expecting to see the mangled remains of his father's body lying across a nearby tree stump. But then, like a gift, he remembered something:

How much wood would a woodchuck chuck
If a woodchuck could chuck wood?

*A woodchuck would chuck all the wood he could chuck
If a woodchuck could chuck wood.*

Since first grade Jimmy had viewed it as nothing more than a silly piece of verse. He now clung to its deeper meanings as though it was one of Shakespeare's greatest works. After all, the poem did *not* say:

*How many dads would a woodchuck chuck
If a woodchuck could chuck dads?*

At the heart of the verse was an obvious but vital truth. Woodchucks ate wood, not people! The more Jimmy turned it over in his mind, the more sense it made. After all, if the creature who had kidnapped his dad was out for blood, wouldn't he have simply gnawed him in two on the spot and left his corpse on 100th Street? No, the woodchuck wanted his father alive. Jimmy gazed over the devastated forest. It was a truly frightening sight. With the exception of their stumps, rows of trees had disappeared, chewed into sawdust and pulp.

"Hey, Jimmy!" William called. "Check it out!"

William and Janice were on their knees in front of a

giant footprint. The ground nearby was covered with hundreds of them.

"So what do we do next?" William asked.

"Next?" Janice said. "We explore."

She put her fingers in her mouth and whistled—loudly. Another hidden talent that could be put to good use during recess, Jimmy thought. Was there anything that Janice couldn't do?

"What are you calling for?" William said. "Won't that attract the chucks to us?"

It was a valid point. Jimmy had been so focused on what the woodchucks had done to the forest that he hadn't concerned himself with two even more important questions: Where were they now, and what would they do if they came back?

Janice whistled again, louder this time. A moment later Jimmy heard the sound of paws moving swiftly across the field. He froze. William had been right! Janice *had* attracted the woodchucks! Terrified, he spun in a slow circle, searching the horizon, fully expecting to see a horde of wild rodents. What he saw instead was just as strange. Three giant Dalmatians, the size of small ponies, sprinted over a hill and pulled to a halt in front of Janice, tails wagging. Jimmy took a step back, his heart pounding. He had always wanted a dog, but not one the size of a small horse.

"Okay, guys," Janice said. "Hop on."

"Hop on?" Jimmy said.

"You've got to be kidding," William said.

"Chill, Mr. President," Janice said. "They don't bite."

To prove her point, she raised her face to the lead dog.

"Here you go," she said. "Good boy."

The lead Dalmatian licked Janice square on the nose.

"Seems friendly enough," William said.

Then the dog barked. Jimmy and William jumped back so quickly that they stumbled and nearly fell. Janice laughed.

"Losers," she said. "That means he likes you."

She snapped her fingers. The lead dog lay down on his stomach. When Janice climbed on his back, the dog rose to all fours.

"Your turn," Janice called down. "Grab a tuft of fur on your dog's neck and hold on."

Janice snapped her fingers again, and the two remaining dogs lay down in front of the boys. William looked at Jimmy, shrugged, and climbed on, leaving Jimmy no choice but to follow suit.

"Whoa," he said. "Easy does it."

The dog glanced back at him, snorted, then faced front,

as if he barely noticed that there was suddenly a boy perched on his back. Jimmy teetered to his side and almost fell off before finding his balance.

"Ready?" Janice said.

"Where to?" Jimmy asked.

"My sources," Janice said. "Maybe one of them saw what happened."

Janice gently nudged her dog with her heels and took off across the ravaged forest at a brisk trot. Jimmy's and William's Dalmatians followed. William was pitched forward, both arms hugging his dog's neck, while Jimmy was frantically reaching for a tuft of hair to keep himself from slipping. Only a last-minute grab for the dog's right ear kept him from sliding to the ground.

"The people of Grindlepick are wonderful with animals," Janice called back, giving her dog another nudge with her heels. "The wild Dalmatians especially. They ride them everywhere."

With that the lead Dalmatian stretched into a gentle lope. Soon Janice and the two boys were riding side by side down a winding dirt road that straddled two cotton candy fields. Yes, the South Forest had been destroyed. Yes, a gang of giant woodchucks was on the loose. But this planet was beautiful! Alongside the colorful cotton fields were ponds, grassy pastures, and stone fences. Behind the fences were cottages, some made of wood, others of stone. The sky was an ever-changing shade of purple. Jimmy could see the dim outlines of Grindlepick's two moons up high.

Janice soon led the boys down another wide dirt road, past cottages and smaller pastures.

"Hmmm," Janice said.

"What?" William asked.

Janice glanced at the boys. "Look around," she said. "I see cottages, but no people."

Jimmy didn't think it was so strange. What kind of person would stick around with a gang of wood-thirsty woodchucks on the loose? Out of the corner of his eye he saw what he thought was another Dalmatian bounding toward them through the tall grass. He blinked. What looked like the fur of a dog was actually the black beard of a small man, no more than three feet tall, holding a large pitchfork. He was moving quickly for someone so little—so quickly, in fact, that Jimmy thought he was on the attack. But just as Jimmy was about to cry, "Run!" the man stopped short and planted the pitchfork in a clump of weeds.

"Is that you, little miss?"

Janice had already dismounted.

"It's good to finally see a familiar face!"

A moment later the girl and man embraced. Jimmy realized that he had never seen Janice so affectionate on Earth.

"This is Simon," she told the boys, pulling away.

"Simon P. McKee the Second!" the man corrected. He scowled. "Your two friends can call me Mr. McKee!"

Jimmy shot William a glance. Simon certainly seemed crabby for someone who had devoted his life to growing candy. Though he knew it was risky to stare at a man armed with a pitchfork, Jimmy couldn't help himself. Simon was just that strange looking. First there were his teeth, worn down to nubs—the result of a lifetime of snacking on cotton candy, Jimmy supposed. Then there was his physique. Though he was so short he barely came up to Janice's neck, Simon's arm muscles were absolutely gigantic, perhaps the result of years of working in the fields. Standing on a pair of spindly legs, he resembled a miniature professional wrestler in desperate need of a dentist.

"Where is everybody?" Janice asked.

Simon spat a wad of what appeared to be blue cotton candy on the ground.

"Evacuated!" he said.

Janice was surprised. "The whole planet?"

Simon nodded and grabbed his pitchfork from the weed clump.

"Those who weren't trampled, anyway. The overgrown rodents came last week just after the frost. They gobbled our trees and sent most everyone running for the hills." Then he grinned, exposing a full view of his decayed molars. "But Simon P. McKee the Second don't scare easy!"

On the word "easy," Simon spat again. Startled, William's dog reared and accidentally flipped his rider onto the ground with a loud *thwap!*

"Hey!" William called.

As Jimmy dismounted to help his friend back to his feet, Simon waved his pitchfork and kept right on talking.

"You want to know why I don't scare easy?" he shouted, now pacing back and forth. "Because I'm a Grindlepicker! I got cotton candy running in my blood! Got the Grindlepick moons in my pores! Got sugar cane in my spit! I'll be chicken whipped with a cold rock if I let a horde of angry rodents drive me off my rightful property!"

For the first time, Jimmy noticed a small stone cottage atop a nearby hill next to a small copse of still-standing trees—Simon's home.

"But where did everyone go?" Janice asked.

Simon waved toward the sky.

"Took the cotton candy barges wherever they could."

Jimmy could no longer restrain himself.

"You didn't happen to see a tall man with one of the woodchucks?" he asked. "From Earth?"

Jimmy never could have anticipated what happened next. Though tiny, Simon moved with surprising speed. In a flash the small man had his pitchfork at Jimmy's throat.

"Man from Earth? You know him?"

Jimmy swallowed hard, too terrified to speak.

"Simon!" Janice said. "Easy!"

Back on his feet, William lunged for Simon's legs. But the man pushed him to the ground as casually as if he were chopping down a cotton candy tuft. He then pushed the pitchfork prongs directly against Jimmy's skin.

"Answer me!"

"Know who?" the boy managed.

"The Earth man! Trying to sell us his Plasta-stuff!"

"Plasta-stuff?" Jimmy said, heart pounding. "The tall man I meant was my father! He's a writer."

Simon blinked. "What?"

"My father!" Jimmy repeated. "Honest!"

"He's serious," Janice said. "Let him go!"

Simon wrinkled his brow and looked at Jimmy. Just like that, his face softened. He lowered the pitchfork.

"So that's why the little squirt is here with you?" he

asked Janice. "A chuck got his daddy?"

Janice nodded. "You didn't see him, did you?"

Simon spat, then shook his head. "No," he said, looking at Jimmy. "Hate to be the one to give you some hard news, boy. But one of those woodchucks got my dad, too. Squashed him flatter than a chicken whipped cotton tuft. If one of them got yours, he's probably dead."

"Dead?" Jimmy gasped. "No, no! It's not true! We would have found his body on the street in New York." He turned to Janice. "Isn't that right?"

Janice was no longer paying attention but looking beyond Simon's house across the horizon.

"Shhh!" she said.

"What?" William said. "I don't hear anything."

"But about my dad," Jimmy said. "You think he's all right?"

"Listen!" Janice hissed.

A distant *thump*, *thump*, *thump* was echoing across the Grindlepick landscape. Suddenly Janice's and Jimmy's Dalmatians began to bark wildly. William's reared again and whinnied.

"Woodchucks!" Simon spat.

"We have to move!" Janice said.

At her sharp whistle the dogs dropped to their stomachs. In a flash the children were on their backs, and Janice brought her dog to Simon's side.

"Get on!" she said. "Hurry!"

But instead of jumping on Janice's Dalmatian, Simon turned toward the coming swarm, eyes glistening.

"Come and get me, you overgrown rodents!" he said, almost to himself. Then louder: "Step on my property and Simon P. McKee the Second is going serve you up a good old-fashioned Grindlepick chicken whipping!"

With that Simon held his pitchfork high, raised his bearded face to the sky, and screamed. Then he was off, sprinting madly toward his home.

"Simon!" Janice cried.

Just like that, the woodchucks appeared over the horizon—six of them. Jimmy shuddered. Running upright on their back legs, the giant rodents were even taller than he had imagined—a good thirty feet each. Their teeth glinted wildly in the bright Grindlepick sun. Their whiskers fanned out from under their noses like spears. And then there was the noise. Along with the *thump, thump* of their paws pounding the ground was the *chomp, chomp* of their powerful jaws and the *slurp, slurp* of their tongues. Clearly this was a pack of rodents on a mission—to destroy everything in their path.

And now Simon was running straight toward them, pitchfork swinging.

"Yaa!" Janice cried.

Her dog ran after Simon at an all-out sprint. Jimmy and William exchanged a glance. Did they stay and help with the rescue, or did they run for their lives?

"Git!" Jimmy said.

"For the United States Senate!" William cried.

With two quick kicks the boys had their Dalmatians chasing after Janice. But they saw their task was hopeless. Simon, who had gotten a good head start, reached his home seconds before the giant rodents. As the first five began to gnaw through Simon's small grove of trees, the biggest one of all—a monster that stood a good twenty feet on all fours—faced the man. It then opened its mouth, exposing two absolutely immense front teeth, larger and sharper than the mightiest harpoons. Simon was un-impressed.

"You don't scare me, you bucktoothed monstrosity!" he yelled, waving his pitchfork in a circle over his head. "I'm Simon P. McKee the Second! This is my land! Now git!"

Though poised to kill, the gargantuan woodchuck seemed surprised, perhaps even a bit amused, by the small Grindlepicker's courage. Simon pressed his advantage.

With a mighty shout he planted his pitchfork in the wood-chuck's front right paw. But instead of convincing the giant rodent that it was in its best interest to leave, the wound only shocked it back into action. With a mighty thump of a giant paw, it squashed Simon flat. As the animal bounded away to feast on the remaining few trees, Janice jumped off her dog and kneeled by his side.

"Simon!" she said.

Drawing near, Jimmy gasped. Smack in the middle of the giant paw print was the Grindlepicker, flattened like a pancake. Had his father come to a similar fate? The thought made Jimmy so sick, he almost fell off his dog. William gently helped Janice to her feet.

"It's terrible," he said. "But we've got to move while we've got the chance!"

"He's right!" Jimmy said.

Even then the woodchucks were demolishing the final standing tree in back of Simon's small cottage. William tried to lead Janice to her waiting Dalmatian. She was crying.

"Hurry!" Jimmy said.

But it was already too late. With a mighty crash the last tree fell to the ground. As the woodchucks began to turn it into pulp, one of the animals decided it was ready for some fun. With four quick leaps it was at the children's side.

With a whoosh it had the bucktoothed girl in its paw.

"Janice!" William cried.

She screamed and kicked the rodent in the chest. She made a fist and punched it in the nose. But it was no use. The woodchuck rose slowly to its hind legs, up, up, up until it stood over thirty feet tall. It then held the struggling girl high in the air and began to toss her back and forth, from one paw to the other.

TEN

Rampaging Woodchucks

JIMMY AND WILLIAM WEREN'T HEROES. NEITHER BOY had ever stood up to a bully or chased a mugger down the street. Perhaps the old Jimmy and William would have run when faced with certain death at the hands of a gang of rampaging woodchucks. But the past day had turned their world upside down.

It was Jimmy who acted first. Yes, as used by Simon P. McKee the Second, the pitchfork had done nothing more than anger an already ferocious woodchuck. But the Grindlepicker had been so angry, he had stabbed the rodent without taking a moment to find the place that would do the most damage. Jimmy didn't make the same mistake. Grabbing the weapon, he noticed a small area halfway up the woodchuck's leg that was unprotected by kneecap or layers of muscle. With the rodent's attention still focused on Janice, the boy took aim and rammed the pitchfork home with all his might.

"Yaaaaa!" he cried.

The woodchuck winced and lurched backward. Which was when William saw his opening. While the pitchfork still dangled out of the rodent's leg, the chubby boy improvised a follow-up attack that no doubt would have made his famous uncle smile. Stepping bravely toward the animal (now hopping furiously up and down on one leg, but still dangling Janice high off the ground), the boy flung himself at the rodent's uninjured leg, opened wide, and took a giant bite. He didn't let go.

The woodchuck's agonized cry echoed down to the cotton candy fields. It sank to its back haunches and tried to shake William off.

"Finish him off, Janice!" Jimmy called.

She took aim with her right index finger and poked the giant rodent hard in the right eye. With that, the mighty chuck rose to its full height and roared. Both paws shot up to its injured eye, and Janice fell to the ground.

"You okay?" Jimmy asked.

"Yeah!"

William ran over, spitting fur out of his mouth. "Let's scram!"

Janice whistled. In seconds the dogs were by their sides.

"Yaaa!" Janice called.

And in a flash the children were mounted and hell-bent for the cotton candy fields, with the five remaining rodents hot on their trail. Worse, the lead chuck already had William in its sights.

"Watch out!" Jimmy called.

The mighty rodent was gaining dangerously. William nudged his dog to the right in the nick of time. The woodchuck dove, somersaulted, then came up coughing out a mouthful of grass. Terrified, William's Dalmatian sprinted to Jimmy's side.

"Close call!" William yelled.

To Jimmy's surprise his friend seemed exhilarated. Then William swung around on his dog and rode backward!

"Come and get us, you ugly mutants!" he cried. "An army of gophers could outrun you any day of the week!"

Jimmy shuddered. He doubted the woodchucks understood English. On the other hand, even the stupidest animal knew when it was being insulted.

"William!" he shouted. "Stop it!"

William flipped forward just as Janice pointed ahead and cried, "Look!"

The light scent of lemon filled the air. Rising before the

three children were the cotton candy fields. Their dogs running side by side, Jimmy and William crouched low, imitating the jockeys they had seen on TV.

"We'll lose 'em in the fields!" Janice called.

There was a brief second when Jimmy allowed himself to believe it. The woodchucks were still coming; but running strong, the Dalmatians had gained ground. Maybe they really would make it back to the ship.

But then he heard it: *Thump, thump, thumpa, thumpa, thump!*

"What's that?" William called.

Jimmy swallowed hard. Before he could answer, a wall of woodchucks burst over an adjacent hill, twenty at least, tongues wagging, teeth glinting.

"To the road!" Janice cried.

She directed her dog onto a dirt pathway that led to the fields. The smell of lemon grew thicker and sweeter with every step.

"Go, boy!" Jimmy called. "You can do it!"

The dogs were running all out, panting hard, not slowing. But how long could they last? Jimmy looked over his shoulder again. Woodchucks dominated the entire skyline—a giant surging army. Suddenly Janice veered off the road to her right.

"Follow me!" she called.

Boom! Her dog crashed into the heart of the cotton candy tufts themselves.

"Where we going?" Jimmy called.

"You'll see!"

For the next minute Jimmy didn't see much. Cotton candy tufts slapped his face hard, even as some of the them ended up in his mouth. Jimmy could hear the panting of the dogs, pushing themselves to their limit, and the *thump, thump* of the woodchucks as they plunged through the field, giving chase. It was all Jimmy could do to hold on. With every step he expected to feel the sharp sting of a claw sinking into his neck. Soon the sound of the woodchucks was so loud that Jimmy glanced over his shoulder. He gasped. They were no more than ten feet behind.

"This way!" Janice said.

She guided her dog into a field of lime cotton candy. But as soon as they entered, Janice directed her dog up a steep incline and back out. Then they were out of the fields altogether, riding next to a small wood. Jimmy blinked.

Woods—with trees!

"Yes!" Janice shouted. "Got it!"

"Got what?" William asked.

"Just keep riding!" Janice commanded. "Into the woods!"

By that point the boys knew enough to do what they were told. Jimmy didn't dare look back. He could feel the heat of the woodchucks' breath. He could hear their wild, frantic squeaking. And there was the ever-present sound of their paws pounding the ground, closer and closer. Soon Janice and the boys had to close their eyes to protect them from the slapping leaves and branches, but the dogs didn't slow down, expertly zigzagging in and out between trees. Finally, to Jimmy's surprise, Janice cried, "Whoa!" The dogs stopped on a dime and turned, panting hard.

"What on earth are you doing?" Jimmy cried.

Janice pointed.

"Look!"

The woodchucks had stopped at the edge of the tree line!

Rip! Snort! Crash!

One tree down!

Gnaw! Crack! Crash!

Then another—and one more after that!

Jimmy had once read the legend of Paul Bunyan, the famous tall-tale hero who was said to chop down a state's worth of trees in a single day. But Paul Bunyan and his ox, Babe, were no match for thirty woodchucks. Janice had guessed right. The animals' primary goal wasn't to kill people. They wanted one thing: wood!

Crack! Crack! Crash!

The trees came down one after another.

"Follow me!" Janice said.

She circled her dog around the outside of the woods. On the edge of the cotton candy fields, Janice stopped again. Without saying a word, the three friends witnessed a horrible but strangely spectacular display of destruction. One by one the woodchucks gnawed down all the trees. Jimmy was struck by their incredible teamwork. While one woodchuck held a tree in place with its massive paws, two others chewed through the trunk, sending wood splintering. When the tree had fallen to the ground, four to six woodchucks—never more or fewer—would gnaw it to bits. Then the group would separate and move on to new trees.

Janice sighed. "Poor Simon just got in their way."

Though he knew there was no answer, Jimmy couldn't resist the next question.

"Do you think he was right about my dad? Do you think he's—?"

He couldn't finish the sentence. Janice looked away, refusing to meet his eyes. But William was ready with an encouraging word.

"Why would a woodchuck want to off your dad, dude? It makes no sense."

For the time being, Jimmy had no choice but to be satisfied with that answer. The thought of his father already dead was too much to bear.

"Back to the ship," Janice said, "before they see us."

With the woodchucks occupied, Janice led the boys back across the cotton candy fields at a gentle lope. There the trio patted and hugged their dogs good-bye, then scrambled up the ramp. As the Dalmatians trotted back into the fields away from the woodchucks, Jimmy, Janice, and William climbed into their barber chairs.

"Strap up," Janice said.

Seconds later the ship began to rise. Hovering over the planet's surface, Jimmy looked out the front window. In the distance the woodchucks were already finishing off the last trees in the woods. He felt a chill.

"Can we get going?" he asked.

Janice grabbed the throttle.

"Hold on!" she said.

Seconds later orange fire shot out of the ship's afterburners. With a mighty whoosh *The Fifth Floor* blasted off, leaving Grindlepick behind.

ELEVEN

Ear Wax and Nostril Hairs

Once Janice had the ship on autopilot, she reached for the control panel.

"Okay," she said. "Time to get more information."

"Finding out more about that Plasta-stuff might give us some answers," William said.

Janice didn't answer. As she busied herself at the controls, the boys had no choice but to sit quietly in their chairs and look out the window. Jimmy tried to remain positive. Yes, they had no concrete leads on his father. On the other hand, despite what had happened to Simon (who, after all, had attacked one of the animals), he had seen proof that the woodchucks' main goal was to eat trees, not people. That had to mean something.

Just then the front screen flickered. For a few seconds the dim image of a purple moon with lava pits filled the screen.

"No, no, no," Janice muttered.

As one of the pits exploded, Jimmy flinched, but with another flicker the image changed—this time to a creature that looked something like an octopus, crawling across a barren desert.

"No, not that," Janice muttered.

With another turn of the dial the octopus dimmed, replaced by the stars outside the ship.

"Okay," Janice said. "Here we go!"

She turned the knob half an inch to the right. Again the stars faded. This time Jimmy could see the grainy image of a man scratching his beard.

"Yes," Janice said. "Got him!'

The man's face filled the entire screen in extreme close-up.

"Henry?" Janice asked.

The man smiled, exposing the telltale mouth of a Grindlepicker—a row of jagged, yellow nubs in place of teeth. His voice came in over the buzz and hiss of static. "I thought it was you, little miss. Sorry for the extreme close-up. My camera's on my watch."

"I'm glad you made it off of Grindlepick," Janice said.

"Just in time, too."

Janice wrinkled her brow. "Were many killed?"

"Luckily most were not," Henry said. "Our cottages are made of stone, not wood."

"But where did the woodchucks come from?" Jimmy asked. "The pods?"

Henry pulled gently on his beard. "That's what we think. A few days ago we had a brief frost."

"And then?" William asked.

Before Henry could answer, the ship began to shake up and down. Lines began to run through the screen, punctuated by loud static.

"Is everything okay?" Jimmy shouted, clutching his barber chair.

"Must be hitting some interstellar waves," Janice said. "We'll be fine."

Just then *The Fifth Floor* bucked and dropped in space. The screen went blank. Moving fast, Janice steadied the ship, then reached under her barber chair and fiddled with a set of wires. In seconds a flurry of green sparks flew out of her control panel, accompanied by a low hiss of steam.

Sitting back up in her chair, she gently finessed a knob on her control panel. Soon the front screen filled with white snow. Just like that, Henry was back.

"So now I'm on this transport," he was saying. Clearly, he didn't know that he had been cut off. "Some of us

Grindlepickers are going to the Orion sector, others to Andromeda, looking for a safe haven. A few guys are headed to Sugarton to get some answers."

"Sugarton?" William asked.

Janice smiled. "Another perfect planet for a chubster like you, Mr. President. The mountains are made of rock candy."

William frowned. Though he knew that he was overweight, he didn't appreciate having it pointed out, especially by a bucktoothed girl. Too hurt to reply, he sucked in his belly and made a vow to lay off the doughnuts—if he ever got home. In the meantime Janice had turned back to the screen.

"Why Sugarton?" she asked.

"The last few of our cotton candy shipments there were returned," Henry explained. "Then we got a distress call from the crown prince. It was hard to make out the message, but we suspect they've been taken over by woodchucks too."

Again Jimmy was unable to restrain himself.

"Do you know anything about a guy from Earth selling some sort of Plasta-stuff?'" Jimmy asked.

To Jimmy's surprise, he was suddenly looking at an extreme close-up of Henry's ear.

"What's going on?" he said.

"Henry's a little bit deaf," Janice explained.

"His watch must also be his communicator," William said. "He's holding it to his ear to hear better."

That was all very well, except that Jimmy could see three hairs growing out of that ear. He even thought he could make out a plug of wax.

"What did you say?" Henry said.

"A guy from Earth!" William shouted. "Have you seen him?"

Before Henry could answer, the screen began to fritz again.

"Henry!" Janice said. "Adjust your camera!"

But it was too late. The screen was filled with snow. Janice slammed her fist onto the console. She then reached under her seat to jiggle more wires. But before she could, Henry reappeared. This time Janice, William, and Jimmy found themselves gazing at a close-up of his nostrils.

"You're right," they heard Henry say. "This camera of mine has seen better days! All fixed now!"

"Could you move your hand?" Janice asked.

"What?"

"Your hand. We're looking up the inside of your left nostril. I can see hairs."

Henry's face filled the screen once again. Now he was

taking a large bite of orange cotton candy.

"That better?"

"Much."

"Sorry, it's a little bit cramped," he said, chewing. "I'm in storage on a cotton barge." He laughed. "As one of the last ones off the planet, I had to eat my way into my seat."

"Oh, God," Janice said.

"What's that mean?" William asked.

Janice explained. "The poor guy's stuffed into a compartment used to ship cotton candy around the universe."

As bad as Jimmy felt for Henry, he was more concerned with getting answers that might lead him to his father before the transmission fritzed out altogether.

"Please," he said. "Do you know anything about a man? From Earth?"

The ship hit another interstellar wave and jerked up and back. Jimmy and William grabbed their seats just in time to keep from falling, as quickly moving parallel lines began to run up and down the screen. Though Henry was speaking, there was too much static to make out what he was saying. Then all of a sudden the children were looking at another angle on his ear. Then his kneecap. Then the screen went black.

Janice pounded the console, flipping switches and

turning knobs. "Hello? Hello, Henry? Henry? Come in!"

Again she ducked under the console, rejiggling the wires, this time sending a wild array of red, blue, and purple sparks flying through the ship. Then *whoosh!* A bright lavender flame shot out of her console. But this time Henry was gone for good, packed away like a bale of cotton, on his way to a distant part of the universe. Furious, Janice kicked the side of her chair.

"So what next?" William asked.

Janice thought a minute, then turned to the boys.

"Hard to say," she said. "We don't have that much to go on."

"We do know one thing, though," Jimmy said. "There were problems on Sugarton."

"Yeah," Janice said. "But he also said it was overrun with woodchucks."

"So what?" William said. "I'll bite them in the legs!"

Janice smiled. "By the way, thanks for saving my life down there, you guys."

William seemed to be fighting a losing battle with a blush.

"No problem," he said quickly. "But listen, Sugarton might be a good next move. Maybe we can find something out."

"Is it nearby?" Jimmy asked.

Janice punched a set of coordinates into her console. Seconds later the front screen was filled with a giant map of the solar system. To Jimmy's dismay, Sugarton was a distant speck in a far corner of the galaxy.

"Close enough," Janice said.

Jimmy blinked. "What? It looks like a forty-year trip."

Janice laughed. "Don't you remember how quickly we got to Grindlepick? In light-years Sugarton is a stroll to the corner store. Strap in!"

TWELVE

Sugarton

JIMMY'S FATHER HAD ONCE JOKED THAT GETTING around New York City by cab took twenty-two minutes no matter what the starting point or destination. By the time Janice's ship reached the outer reaches of Sugarton, Jimmy had begun to think that getting from planet to planet in the solar system took exactly half an hour. *The Fifth Floor* was just that fast. Still, Jimmy discovered that half an hour could feel like a very long time. Throughout the flight he did his best to convince himself that his father was safe. But time and again his thoughts were invaded by the image of Simon P. McKee the Second, squashed flatter than a cockroach. Worse, with William studiously copying passages from *Light Speed and You* into his binder and Janice busy at the controls, Jimmy had no one to distract him. After what seemed like an eternity, Janice turned back from her console.

"Almost there!" she said.

Out the front screen was a bright orange dot.

"That's X-9," Janice said. "One of Sugarton's eleven moons."

The news was sufficiently interesting to tear William away from Janice's book.

"Eleven moons?" he said.

The girl nodded. "None are colonized yet, but there's talk of opening a taffy mine on X-3."

Jimmy wrinkled his brow. "Does every planet or moon in the solar system make candy?"

Janice grinned. "I'm very selective."

She inched the steering wheel to the right, maneuvering the ship past X-9. Up close, Jimmy could see its barren landscape and deep craters, broken up by tall jagged peaks.

"See those mountains?" Janice said as they flew over one of the taller ranges. "They're nothing compared to what's on Sugarton."

She directed the ship to the left of X-9, and the planet came into view. From a distance it looked a little bit like Earth. Underneath a haze of clouds, blocks of brown-and-green land were separated by larger blocks of blue water. But while the planet looked familiar, its moons left no doubt that they were in an altogether different part of the universe.

Three floated to its left, one red, one green, one purple. To its right were four more, two yellow, and two light blue.

"Nice, huh?" Janice said.

She grinned back at the boys, once again enjoying her role as tour guide of the universe. The sight was so stunning that Jimmy temporarily forgot about the possible danger that awaited them on the planet's surface. But if William was taken by Sugarton's beauty, he didn't show it. His interest lay in the ship's mechanics.

"Wait," he said, pencil poised over his binder. "How do we break into the planetary atmosphere without burning up?"

"Hypergloss chrome-plated shields" was the answer.

"But how do you calibrate the exact right angle at which to enter a planet's atmosphere?"

Janice sighed. "The retro-flux inverter does it. It's all on page eighty-four."

As William flipped eagerly to the page in question, Jimmy smiled. To his surprise, his friend had willingly accepted his role as Janice's student. Even more, it appeared that William was actually getting to like her. It was hard to believe, but Jimmy had to admit that he was getting to like Janice too. One thing was certain: She knew how to fly a spaceship.

"All right, guys," she said a few moments later. "I'm taking her in."

Sugarton's blues, greens, and whites grew larger and larger until they took up the entire front screen. Suddenly the ship began to shake violently. But with Janice holding the wheel steady, *The Fifth Floor* slipped easily into Sugarton's upper atmosphere, and they were soon soaring through a pale purple sky, over a spread of orange clouds. The planet's three remaining moons, all greenish blue, rose over the far horizon. It was a sight so unexpected that William actually let his binder slide to the floor.

"Cool," he said.

"Just wait," Janice replied.

The ship dropped through an orange cloud. When they whooshed out the other side, the boys gasped. Before them was a towering series of mountain ranges that rose, peak upon peak upon peak, high into the purple sky. More striking, each summit was covered with layers of glittering crystal so bright that they had to squint.

"Are these the rock candy mountains?" Jimmy asked.

Janice nudged the ship down underneath the lowest layer of clouds that surrounded the peaks. There the boys saw workers dressed in thick fur coats, standing on wooden platforms, chipping at crystals with ice picks.

"Rock candy miners," Janice said. "They work the mountains every spring and summer. The crystals regenerate in the fall and winter."

As they were swooping by, one of the miners waved.

"Okay," Janice said. "Let's look around."

A drop in altitude, and the crystal formations gave way to a series of waterfalls. Lower still, the mountains turned to gray and white rock; then the ship was gliding over a series of wide grassy pastures, dotted with small homes and barns. Though the land was beautiful, it wasn't long before the three travelers began to feel uneasy. Jimmy said it first.

"Where are the trees?"

"And how about the people?" William said.

As if on cue, a grassy field below them turned suddenly into a vast expanse of stumps, roots, and sawdust. Worse, the view out the front screen showed that the devastation went on for miles. There was only one tree left standing as far as the eye could see. Jimmy's heart sank.

"Looks like your friend Henry was right," he said to Janice. "The chucks were here."

Janice and William didn't have the heart to answer. With each passing stump, the crew grew more discouraged. Had they escaped the overgrown rodents on Grindlepick only to fall prey to them on Sugarton?

The last thing Jimmy wanted to do was land. But how else was he going to find his father?

"I guess we should snoop around and see what we can find out," he said halfheartedly.

Janice cut the engine over a small field of grass. But just as the ship was starting to descend, Jimmy noticed something out the front screen.

"No! Go a little farther!"

Janice turned. "Why?"

"Up ahead!" Jimmy pointed. "Trees!"

Indeed, up ahead was a wall of them—not just three or four, either, but a row that stretched across the horizon. Janice nudged the throttle, and a moment later the crew was flying over a forest. The trees were so thick with leaves, it was impossible to see the ground.

"This is weird," Janice said.

"What do you think happened?" Jimmy asked.

"Maybe the chucks got full?" William said. "Maybe they're down there right now gearing up for another meal."

Jimmy shuddered, thinking back to the chilling *thump, thump, thump* of the Grindlepick woodchucks closing in for the kill. When he'd stabbed the giant rodent in the knee, he'd felt like he could conquer the world. He now realized how lucky he was to be alive. But just as he was beginning to imagine how it would feel to be carried up the Sugarton mountains in the mouth of a particularly murderous woodchuck, he noticed something.

"Hey, look," he said. "The trees."

"I am looking," William said. "A tree is a tree."

"No, look at how they're spaced," Jimmy said. "One after another after another in perfect rows."

It was true. Though it was hard to see through the thick branches, each trunk was the exact same distance from the one before and after it.

"Hmmm," Janice wondered.

Just then *The Fifth Floor* reached what appeared to be some sort of construction site. By the edge of the forest sat a giant crane with four metal arms. Fifty feet away stood a pale orange rectangular building the size of four basketball courts. Most striking of all was a giant hose, a good four feet around, that stuck out of the building's side and snaked its way to the forest. Workers in blue jumpsuits milled about, seeing to the hose and crane or simply waiting for orders.

"What in the world is this?" William asked.

"Let's get a better look," Janice said.

She cut the engine, and the ship was soon hovering three hundred feet or so above the ground. The children pressed to the front screen.

"They're Grindlepickers!" William cried.

"Do you think they've been kidnapped?" Jimmy asked.

"And enslaved?" Janice said.

Suddenly, four giant woodchucks moved silently out of the forest. To the children's amazement, there were bits in their mouths and harnesses around their heads. Sitting on each woodchuck's back, holding the reins, was an enormous man with a flowing beard and a light blue cloak. Perched on the men's heads were giant purple Viking helmets.

"Vikings?" William said. "Riding *woodchucks*?"

What happened next was so out of the ordinary, the children couldn't quite believe it. The Viking on the largest woodchuck—a mammoth man with a red beard—waved his arms and gave a command. A group of ten Grindlepickers pushed the giant crane closer to the edge of the forest. With a belch of smoke, the crane's four arms picked up the enormous hose, flipped it upside down, and pressed its opening against the ground. Then a stream of about a hundred Grindlepickers hurried out of the building and lined up on either side of the hose. After that the red-bearded Viking barked another command. Plumes of smoke rose out of the building's windows. The hose began to pulsate, twitch, and finally, as the workers did their best to hold it in place, shake back and forth like a snake gone mad. Just like that, the end of the hose shot into the air, revealing a perfectly formed tree trunk! Without missing a beat the hose began to move down the line like the needle on a sewing machine, touching the ground, then shooting straight up, making tree after tree after tree!

"This is crazy!" Jimmy said. "They're making a new forest!"

It was true. Below, another group of Grindlepickers was throwing ladders against the newly created tree trunks. Seconds later they were climbing up, then attaching branches and leaves to the sides of the trees.

"Insane!" William said.

"Yes," Janice said. "Why gnaw down the trees only to replace them with fakes?"

It was a good question, but the three travelers would have to wait for an answer. In their eagerness to view the construction site, they had forgotten to remain hidden. The Viking on the smallest woodchuck noticed them first and motioned to the leader. By the time the children realized what had happened, everyone on the ground was looking up. Redbeard barked a command, and the four arms of the crane lifted the giant hose high in the air, pointing it straight at *The Fifth Floor*!

Janice's eyes went wide.

"Time to show me what you're made of, guys," she called. "Battle stations!"

THIRTEEN

A Homicidal Maniac?

JANICE FLIPPED A SWITCH ON HER CONSOLE. Viewfinders dropped from the ceiling in front of the three barber chairs; firing mechanisms with triggers flipped out of the seats' arms.

"Wow!" William said. "I didn't know you had missiles hooked up on this thing!"

"Environmentally sensitive solar-powered lasers," Janice replied. "Come on! In your seats!"

As the crew dove for their chairs, a giant tree exploded out of the hose. Spinning like a missile, it shot straight toward them.

"Incoming!" Janice cried.

Jimmy shuddered. After a day that had included everything from flying in spaceships to sprinting Dalmatians, was his adventure to be brought to an end by a tree?

"Got it!" Janice cried.

She looked through the viewfinder, locked the tree in the crosshairs, and squeezed the trigger. A red beam shot out of a portal on the bottom of the ship. But it went wide.

"Missed!" she cried.

With the tree seconds away from impact, there was no time to think. Heart pounding, Jimmy looked through his viewfinder. In a flash he set it in his crosshairs and pulled the trigger. The next thing Jimmy knew, sawdust and bits of broken wood were smashing against the front screen.

"You nailed it!" William called.

Jimmy pumped his fist, but there was no time to celebrate. Another tree was already on its way.

"Hold off, guys!" William cried. "This baby's mine!"

He looked through the viewfinder, then pumped the height bar on his seat. Up high, he took another look, then lowered the chair back down.

"Shoot already!" Janice cried.

In response William pumped his seat back up to full height.

"William!" Jimmy shouted.

The boy finally fired. The red laser shot out the bottom of *The Fifth Floor*, but it hit the tree on one end, not its middle. Instead of exploding, the tree flipped sideways and began to spin like a windmill. Now it was coming even faster! Luckily, Jimmy and Janice were ready. While it was harder to hit a spinning target, they lined up the center of the tree in their crosshairs, took aim, and fired. Two environmentally sensitive solar lasers found their marks, and the tree shattered. A largish chunk of the lower trunk smacked against the front screen, but *The Fifth Floor* survived intact.

Jimmy jumped up, fists clenched. "Yes!"

William looked back through his viewfinder. "William H. Taft the Fifth is ready! Bring it on!"

"That may not be necessary," Janice said. "Look!"

To their surprise, the four-armed crane was lowering the hose back to the ground.

"They're giving up!" William said.

He was so excited, he shimmied across the room, doing a belly dance.

"What next?" he called. "I say we head on down and free the Grindlepickers!"

There was a moment when the brave crew believed it possible; a few short seconds when they all thought they could swoop out of the sky dodging tree missiles, woodchucks, and Vikings, gather the hundred or more Grindlepickers in their small ship, and whoosh into the sky. But the moment passed, and the children soon saw that their troubles were just beginning. Redbeard hadn't given up but simply changed tactics. As the children were celebrating, a plume of smoke rose under the giant rectangular building. A moment later the building lifted off the ground! Janice saw it first.

"Uh-oh," she yelled. "We've got a space barge!"

Once it got airborne, the barge rose with surprising speed. Janice dove for her controls, but before she could throw *The Fifth Floor* into gear, the enemy ship was at its side. Jimmy and William were stunned. It was astonishing that anything so big—it was two city blocks wide and a good fifty feet high—could actually get in the air.

"I'm not waiting around to see what they want," Janice said, hand on the throttle. "Strap in!"

Jimmy and William took a step toward their seats. But then the two friends saw something so surprising that they stopped dead in their tracks. Printed on the ship's side, in large block lettering, was a single word:

PLASTAWOOD

Eyes wide, William and Jimmy exchanged a glance.

"That's the Plasta-stuff Simon was talking about!" William said. "It has to be!"

Jimmy nodded. "I bet it's the stuff they're using to make the fake trees!"

Janice was staring out the front screen, utterly motionless, eyes wide.

"Janice?"

No response.

"Hey, Janice!"

Then he saw it. A side door on the barge had slid open, revealing the barrel of an enormous cannon—aiming directly at them!

"Plastawood?" Janice repeated, half to herself.

Jimmy didn't bother to answer. He jumped for the ship's throttle and rammed it forward. With a loud whoosh *The Fifth Floor* careened downward just as the cannon fired with a thunderous boom! That was all it took to snap Janice back to the present. Jimmy's quick thinking had saved them, but now the ship was at full thrust, angling straight for the trees!

"Watch it!" she called, and dove for the altitude control. With a high-pitched whine, the ship lurched back up just as—boom!—a second cannon shot soared under them and exploded in the forest.

Once Janice got *The Fifth Floor* revved up, it easily outran the giant barge. Moments later the ship was thundering past the famed Sugarton mountains. Soon it exploded back into outer space.

"What're you doing?" William said. "We have to go back and free the Grindlepickers!"

"What about getting clues to my dad?" Jimmy asked. "Wasn't that the point?"

If Janice was listening, she didn't show it. When the ship was safely past X-9, she took it to light speed. Only when *The Fifth Floor* was safely on automatic pilot did she face the boys.

"We'll have better luck tracking your dad from Earth," she said to Jimmy. Then to William, "Also freeing the Grindlepickers."

"Really?" Jimmy said. He was confused. "You found a clue?"

William wrinkled his brow. "What happened up there, Janice? You zoned out."

For a moment the bucktoothed girl was silent, staring out the front screen at the stars. As eager as they were for answers, the boys let her work through her thoughts. She looked strangely sad. Then she shook her head.

"This is going to sound bizarre," she said, "but it would seem that my father might well be a homicidal maniac bent on controlling the universe."

It seemed a strange time to joke around. But Janice was dead serious.

"You're kidding," William said with a laugh. "Your dad? No one ever said anything about him."

"He makes mute buttons, for crying out loud," Jimmy said.

"As a trained scientist I can't overlook facts," she said. "Have you met my father? He is pretty weird."

"Weird maybe," Jimmy said. "But that doesn't mean he's using giant woodchucks to destroy planets."

"I know it doesn't," Janice said.

"Then what?" William said. "This doesn't add up at all."

Janice looked out the front screen, gathering herself. She then adjusted the automatic pilot and turned back to the boys. "About a month ago when I was drawing initial designs for a new retro-flux engine, I went to my dad's office looking for some graph paper. When I got there, I noticed something in the trash—a memo or something. He never leaves anything out like that, so I picked it up. On top of the paper was the word 'Plastawood'—and in the exact same font and color as the logo on the giant barge."

Jimmy and William exchanged a glance. It was suddenly looking as though Henrick Claytooth was up to more in his spare time than collecting corks. It was bad enough that Janice's mother had died from a plunge into the seal pond. But now the girl had discovered that her only remaining parent was criminally insane.

"So what do we do when we get back?" William asked. "Call the police?"

"Yeah, that'd be great," Jimmy said. "We'll just tell them to arrest Janice's dad because we think he might be using giant woodchucks to destroy candy planets, enslave their populations, and take over the universe. They'll get right on it."

William frowned. "It was just a suggestion." He looked at Janice. "What if we go through your dad's desk? Maybe we can find what this Plastawood thing is."

"Right," Jimmy said. "And why they were building a fake forest on Sugarton."

"We might also find clues that lead to Jimmy's father," William said.

Janice nodded. "We might," she said. "But it won't be easy. My father keeps his desk locked, and he never leaves anything out. That's why the memo caught my eye in the first place."

"Then where does he work during the day?" Jimmy said. "Maybe he has another office we can search?"

Janice sat back in her seat. "To tell the truth, I don't know where he goes. I barely ever see him."

Jimmy felt a strong urge to give Janice a hug.

"So tonight we'll search his home office, and tomorrow morning we'll follow him," William said. "And in the meantime we'll warn people."

"Warn people?" Janice said.

"About the woodchucks!" William said. "They've already massacred at least two planets and enslaved the Grindlepickers! Earth is probably next!"

It was an obvious point, but one that Jimmy hadn't even considered. Of course Earth had to be next. He had no desire for his mother and sister to spend the rest of their lives building fake forests on other planets.

"But who's going to believe us?" he asked.

"Maybe no one," William said. "But we've got to try, right?"

Jimmy sighed. Despite experiencing a lifetime's worth of adventure in a single day, he still didn't feel any closer to finding his father. On the other hand, what were their options? To go back to Sugarton and take on an army of woodchucks and a cannonball-shooting flying barge?

"You in, Jimmy?" William asked.

The boy nodded. "Yeah," he said. "Let's go home."

With that, the three friends strapped in. On they flew, down to Earth, bearing a burden they hadn't asked for, but one they accepted without hesitation. Some children are asked to take out the trash. Others are asked to make their beds. Janice, Jimmy, and William had been called upon to do something noble, something important: to make the world safe from woodchucks.

FOURTEEN

Call to the White House

I T WAS JUST AFTER DUSK WHEN JANICE GUIDED *THE Fifth Floor* back over the roof of her building. With a few bumps and hisses, the ship settled slowly into its berth. As the roof closed, the floor and ceiling retracted, along with the barber chair consoles. In a matter of minutes Jimmy found himself back in an ordinary attic.

"How do you feel?" Janice asked.

The boys exchanged a glance.

"Fine, I guess," William said.

"So what next?" Jimmy said. "Check your dad's desk?"

"Fine by me," Janice said. "Maybe we'll get lucky right off the bat."

Though the door to Henrick Claytooth's private third floor office was open, every drawer in his desk was locked and every closet sealed, just as Janice had said it would be.

139

This time the trash can was empty. And there was no tell-tale art on the walls—not even so much as a calendar.

"Does he spend any time in here at all?" Jimmy asked.

Janice shrugged. "Not much." She sat on her dad's desk. "Looks like we'll need to follow him and figure out where he really works."

"Which means we can't find out anything until the morning," Jimmy said.

"But in the meantime we can do something else," Janice said.

"What?' Jimmy said.

She jumped off her father's desk and smiled. "Who wants to call the White House?"

Moments later the threesome was camped out in Janice's room. In the end, using a logic Jimmy couldn't quite follow, William and Janice had elected him to be the one to make the call. Now he was leaning back on some pillows on Janice's bed as William Googled "The White House, Washington, D.C." and jotted down the main number.

"Ready?" he asked.

"Ready enough," Jimmy answered.

Though he tried to sound casual, his heart was racing. It wasn't every day that he talked with the president. Janice dialed and passed him the phone. At the first ring, he stood. At the second, he began to pace. Then came a click and a voice.

"Hello, White House."

Before he said a single word, Jimmy could see that this was going to be difficult.

"Uh, yes," he stammered. "Could you please connect me to the president?"

"The president?" the operator said. To Jimmy's surprise, his voice was expressionless.

"May I ask what this is in reference to?"

Jimmy put his hand over the receiver and turned to his friends. "The president probably gets hundreds of calls a day. What should I say?"

"Say it's a natural disaster," Janice said. "A category five hurricane."

"No, mention Godzilla," William said. "They'll listen to that."

But then Jimmy got his own idea about how to get the president's attention.

"I'd like to report a possible terrorist attack."

"Oh, I see. Is it a bomb threat?"

"Something like that."

"Have you called your local police precinct?"

Clearly the operator was experienced at directing calls

away from the commander in chief to other agencies. Jimmy swallowed.

"We want to spread the word as quickly as possible." He then decided that a dash of the dramatic might help. "Like I said, there are terrorists. Lots and lots of very large, angry terrorists."

Something in the silence on the other end of the line told Jimmy that the man was about to either hang up or connect him to the police.

"Wait," he said.

"Yes?"

Clearly, the operator was giving him one last chance to take his best shot. With no other choice, Jimmy jumped in.

"Okay, here's the real story. I just got back from Grindlepick—that's where they make all the cotton candy in the universe."

"Hmmm," the operator said. "Do they grow it in fields?"

Jimmy paused. "Uh, yeah," he stammered. "As a matter of fact, they do."

The operator sighed. "I always thought someone should make coffee-flavored cotton candy."

"What's going on?" Janice whispered.

Jimmy put a hand over the mouthpiece. "He wants to know if Grindlepick makes coffee-flavored cotton candy."

"Who?" William asked. "The president?"

"No, the operator!"

"Tell him yes," Janice said. "In the western part of the planet. The light from Grindlepick's second moon helps it grow better."

Jimmy nodded and repeated the information to the operator.

"Interesting," the man said. "Go on."

Was it possible that this man was actually taking him seriously?

"So here's the deal," Jimmy went on. "We flew to Grindlepick to track down these giant woodchucks that had kidnapped my dad. When we got there, there was this whole team of massively large rodents chowing down on the trees."

"Sounds serious."

"It is serious!" Jimmy cried. "Then when we got to Sugarton, they were using enslaved Grindlepickers to make a fake forest! We think this stuff called Plastawood has something to do with it. Anyway, they've already destroyed at least two planets! Probably more, and Earth might be next! That's why we have to warn the president!"

By the time he was finished, Jimmy was breathless.

"Okay," the man said. "Let me connect you."

Jimmy turned to his friends. "He's connecting me!"

William clenched his fists and said, "Yes!"

"Let's put him on speaker!"

She pressed a button on the phone just as someone picked up.

"Hello?"

Jimmy swallowed hard.

"Uh, yes, Mr. President."

But the three friends soon recognized the disembodied voice of a prerecorded message.

"Welcome to the Washington, D.C., Mental Health Agency. Please stay on the line, and a trained professional will be with you shortly."

Jimmy clicked the phone off and sighed.

"That stinks," William said.

"I had a feeling that was going too well," Jimmy muttered.

But things were about to get much worse, for Janice anyway. Just then Angelina barged into the room, doubled over with laughter. She was shaking so hard, she was having trouble standing up.

"Get out!" Janice said. "We're taking care of serious business!"

"Serious business?" Angelina was practically gasping

for breath. "Oh, I'm sure! Like saving Grindlepoop from a bunch of giant man-eating gophers! Or saving the slaves from Boogerton with Plastagunk! God! I can't wait to tell the girls at school about this!"

While Jimmy and William were mildly embarrassed—after all, they knew how it must sound—Janice was furious.

"I've told you a million times, Angelina!" she said. "STOP SNOOPING!"

Janice was right up in her sister's face. But Angelina was unimpressed.

"So who are you guys going to call next?" she asked, stepping away from her sister. "The King of Mongolia? Wait! I know! How about Obi Wan Kenobi! He can lend you another spaceship!"

That was all Janice could take. To Jimmy and William's surprise, she threw herself at her sister's legs and tackled her onto the bed. Seconds later she was walking Angelina to the door in a headlock.

"If you snoop again, I'll smash in your teeth!"

Angelina giggled. "I'd do the same to you, except it might improve your looks."

Janice pushed Angelina into the hall, slammed the door, then kicked a pillow across the room.

"I HATE HER!" she said. "Who cares if she has straight

teeth—she's the one who's stupid. STUPID AND MEAN!"

Stupid and mean seemed like an understatement. Jimmy thought affectionately of Imogene.

"I should have sat on her," William said.

Then Jimmy thought of something.

"If you don't mind my asking," he said, "why did your father get Angelina's teeth fixed and not yours?"

"Yeah," William said. "That doesn't seem fair."

Janice sighed. "If you can believe it, Angelina's teeth used to be even more bucked than mine. But she was already in braces when my mom died."

"So?" Jimmy asked. "What does that have to do with you?"

"Lots, unfortunately," Janice said. She leaned back against the wall. "The only thing I can come up with is that my dad misses my mom so much, he likes having me look exactly like her."

"So what are you saying?" William asked. "He won't get you braces?"

"It's not that simple," Janice said. "He's never offered, but at the same time I've never asked." She paused. "I guess I sort of like looking like my mom, buckteeth and all. The trouble is . . . I think it's hard for Dad to spend time with me because, well, I remind him of her."

The boys exchanged a glance. With each new detail Janice's story got sadder and sadder.

"Well, for what it's worth," William said huskily, "I like your teeth."

Jimmy raised his eyebrows. Janice looked away. Was she embarrassed? It was hard to tell. In seconds she was once again all business.

"Okay, back to work."

Over the next half hour they tried the mayor of New York, two state senators, the metro desk at *The New York Times*, the editorial page at *The Daily News*, four firehouses, the manager of the Mets, the city sanitation commissioner, and the cell phone of a hot dog vendor on 57th Street. Each attempt to spread the word of the coming woodchuck attack turned into a version of Jimmy's call to the White House. After one or two questions, the person on the other line either hung up or connected them to the police.

"So much for warning the world," William said, after striking out on their final try, a captain of the Staten Island ferry.

Jimmy felt thoroughly disheartened. Deep down he had known that the odds of anyone believing them were slim. Still, he had hoped that there would be someone out there with enough imagination to take them seriously.

"I guess it really is up to us alone," Janice said.

"Yep," Jimmy said. "Guess so."

It was a scary thought. Still, Jimmy felt strangely happy. What other ten-year-old boy had the fate of the world placed squarely on his shoulders? It was the ultimate challenge, but one that would have to wait until morning. Suddenly Jimmy felt incredibly sleepy.

"Okay," he said. "So we'll meet here in the morning."

"Seven A.M., sharp," Janice said.

William groaned. "I'll set my alarm clock."

Jimmy smiled. He had his own personal alarm clock— Imogene.

Moments later the boys were saying good-bye at the front door.

"Good-bye," said Janice, and smiled—a wide, buck-toothed grin. "See you guys in the morning."

Jimmy could only imagine what his friends at school would say if they knew he had actually spent an afternoon with Janice Claytooth.

ON THE SHORT WALK HOME, JIMMY COULDN'T STOP himself from hoping. Perhaps the woodchuck had taken a sniff of his father and realized that his dad wasn't made of wood? Maybe his father had told the giant rodent one of his stories and charmed it into releasing him? Maybe Jimmy had just dreamed the entire thing? Inserting the key in the front door of his family's apartment, he said a final prayer.

"Please!" he thought. "Please! Let him be home!"

But when he pushed the door open, it was Imogene who rushed down the hallway and jumped into his arms. His father was nowhere to be seen. Jimmy held his sister tight.

"Hey, Genie," he said. "It's good to see you!"

His mother was thrilled to see him in one piece. But she was angry. Jimmy knew why, of course. He had been gone all afternoon without telling her where he was. On the other hand, cell service was hard to come by in outer space.

"Jimmy!" she said sharply. "You had me worried out of my mind."

"Mommy drink tea," Imogene said.

Now Jimmy felt awful. His mother drank mint tea only when she was really upset.

"I'm sorry, Mom," he said.

Before he could go on, his mother threw her arms around his shoulders and cried.

"I thought something had happened to you."

Jimmy was put into the uncomfortable position of having to comfort his own mother.

"Hey, Mom," he said. "It's okay. Guess what—I have a lead."

His mother wiped her eyes. "You do?"

Jimmy nodded. "Yeah, but you'd better sit down. It's weird."

Before he could tell the story, though, Jimmy noticed Imogene picking up his Game Boy. Strangely a joystick stuck out from its middle.

"Genie?" he asked.

"I fix it!" she called.

With that the girl flicked the joystick. Something amazing happened: The remote floated off the bookshelf! Even more incredibly, as Imogene moved the stick in a circle, the remote moved in a circle too, floating around the room, then settling back on the bookshelf. Of all the things Jimmy had seen that day, it was perhaps the most surprising.

"How in the world did you do that?" he asked.

Imogene tossed the Game Boy on the sofa and began to sing.

"Let's go fly a kite! Up to the highest height!"

"Mom?" Jimmy asked.

Emma shrugged. "She's been fiddling with it all afternoon. She used your father's tool kit."

Jimmy stared at Imogene. Was his little sister

another Janice Claytooth?

"Forget the Game Boy," Emma said. "Now tell me where you've been. And what's this about a lead on your father?"

Seconds later Jimmy's mother was on the sofa with Imogene in her lap. In much the same way that he had told the White House operator, Jimmy took a deep breath and let the story out. When it was over, Imogene squirmed off of her lap and ran to her brother's side.

"Visit the candy!"

Jimmy smiled. "Sure, Genie. Maybe soon."

"You're telling the truth?" his mother asked. She looked at him sharply. "This isn't the time for stories!"

"Come on, Mom," Jimmy said. "Would I lie about something as important as Dad?"

His mother shook her head. "No, I guess not." She paused and wiped away another tear. She stood up. "So let's get you dinner and then to bed. I guess I'll have to set my alarm for six tomorrow."

"Why?" Jimmy said. "Imogene always wakes me anyway."

Again his mother looked annoyed. For a moment Jimmy thought he had done something really wrong.

"James Weathers!" she said. "If you think I would let my only son out of the house to save the world without a good breakfast, you're out of your mind!"

The Ramble

EARLY THE NEXT MORNING, AFTER A BREAKFAST OF blueberry pancakes and bacon—his favorite—Jimmy kissed his mother and Imogene good-bye and headed out. Snow covered parts of the sidewalk and was piled high on the tops of parked cars. Zipping up his winter coat, Jimmy turned down 100th Street. As planned, William was already in front of Emma's Tea.

"Hey," Jimmy said.

"Hey," was the reply.

"You ready?" Jimmy asked.

William held out a bag of doughnuts. Though he'd already had breakfast, Jimmy chose a chocolate glazed. The two friends were soon heading down Columbus Avenue, sharing the sidewalk with early-morning dog walkers and workers returning home after the night shift. Though the walk to Janice's brownstone took a good fifteen minutes, the two boys were too caught up with thoughts of the day ahead to talk. Only when they approached 85th Street did William finally break the silence.

"This is it, huh?" he said. "Save-the-world day?"

"Yeah," Jimmy said.

On 85th Street the boys picked up the pace. Now that the silence had been broken, William began to talk.

"Could you believe Janice's ship? You know, I stayed up half the night reading her book. It's insane. No wonder it's sold only one copy on Earth. She's too brilliant for this planet."

Jimmy grinned. "You like her."

The chubby boy looked like he'd suddenly found a piece of bad liver in his doughnut. For a moment it seemed as if he was going to deny it. But he was cornered.

"Well, sure, I like her," he said. "As a colleague in space exploration."

"Colleague?" Jimmy said. "Then why did you tell her you like her teeth? Why is your face red?"

Just then Jimmy saw something out of the corner of his eye. Without saying a word, he pulled William behind a garbage can.

"What?" William said.

Jimmy pointed down the block at a tiny man wearing a black overcoat, snow boots, and furry red earmuffs who was walking down the steps of the Claytooth brownstone. With the exception of a bald head and slightly bigger nose, he bore a striking resemblance to Angelina.

"That's him!" Jimmy called. "The man in the picture in Janice's hallway!"

Henrick Claytooth moved briskly up 85th Street. The boys saw that they would have to hustle to keep up.

As they passed the brownstone, Janice ran down the steps and fell in beside them.

"Sorry," she said. "He left even earlier than usual."

"Glad we caught him," Jimmy said.

William nodded hello and held out the bag of dough-nuts. Janice selected a jelly-filled and took a bite. By that time Henrick had reached the corner of Central Park West and was waiting for the light. The kids huddled behind a car.

"I wonder if he takes a bus to work," Jimmy said.

"Maybe he walks to midtown?" William said.

"We're about to find out," Janice said.

With the light green, Henrick hurried across the street. But to the children's surprise, he didn't walk to the bus stop at 84th Street. Instead he kept right on walking, moving up a path directly into the park.

"Maybe he works on the East Side?" Jimmy said.

"And walks there through this mushy snow?" William asked.

Jimmy shrugged. "Some people like to walk to work."

"Let's move," Janice said, "before we lose him."

With the light blinking red, the trio ran across the street, then followed Henrick up the path. They were right to hurry. Moving quickly down the side of the road that circles the park's interior, Henrick had picked up his pace. For the next few minutes the children followed him, half walking, half jogging, while occasional cars and cabs moved by. They tried to stay on the cement, but there were times when they were forced to negotiate an unshoveled dirt path. It wasn't long before their boots and pants were soaked. At 79th Street Henrick slipped and pitched sideways into a snow-bank. Without missing a beat, he stood up and walked on without so much as taking a moment to brush himself off.

"Boy," Jimmy said. "Somebody's in a hurry!"

But where was he hurrying to? To look for a site to lay out more pods? To meet the woodchuck that had kid-napped his father? Or was this walk through the snow purely innocent? Maybe Henrick was doing nothing more than taking the long way to work? Jimmy couldn't imag-ine how foolish he would feel if Henrick suddenly ducked out of the park and into an office building.

"What do you think?" Jimmy asked.

"He's got woodchuck written all over him," William said.

"Yeah?"

"It's looking suspicious, all right," Janice said.

Jimmy had to agree. Then Henrick did something even stranger. They were a few blocks below 79th Street. Henrick suddenly plunged off the road—directly into the tree line.

"Wait," Jimmy said. "Isn't that the Ramble?"

It was the most densely wooded part of the park, a mix of twisting paths where all New Yorkers had gotten lost at least once in their lives.

"This is getting seriously weird," William said.

"Let's not lose him now," Janice said.

The children hustled up the road, then followed Henrick down a narrow path into the snowy woods. Instantly, the whirr of city traffic disappeared. The only sound was the *crunch, crunch* of boots on the wet snow. Icicles hung from the tops of tall pines and oaks. Everything was white.

"It's like we're in Narnia or something," William said.

Jimmy half expected to see a faun skip toward them through the snow. But the only other person there was

Henrick. Not that he was easy to see. The Ramble was so thick with trees, and the path so curvy, that the children had to hurry to keep him in sight. Even though everything was covered with wet snow, Henrick kept moving quickly.

Soon the path sloped downward. Then it pushed back up before making its jagged way around a corner and over a stream. After that it wended its way back up, up, up through the snowy woods. Just when Jimmy began to worry that he didn't have the energy to keep going for much longer, something strange happened. As the children rounded a corner, they saw that Henrick was no longer alone. Rather, he was talking to a largish man in a long blue cloak. After another few steps, the children saw exactly who the man was: Redbeard! Quickly they ducked behind a fallen tree.

The Viking was doing most of the talking, gesturing broadly with his hands.

"I wonder if he's bringing your dad up to date on what's happening on Sugarton," William said.

"I doubt they're discussing mute buttons," Janice said.

And just like that, the two men hiked up a steep, snowy slope, directly through the line of trees. The kids followed. The snow was slick, and each of the children slipped once. When they finally reached the hill's crest, their hearts dropped. Henrick and the Viking were nowhere to be seen!

"Where are they?" Jimmy asked.

Janice pointed. The footprints led to a nearby oak.

"There!"

They plunged down the hill and sprinted as best they could, following the footprints to the base of the tree. At the giant oak they looked around.

"This is impossible!" Janice said.

William was staggered. "People can't just disappear, can they?"

Jimmy leaned against the tree, winded and confused. "No—they have to be somewhere nearby."

Or did they? With the strange events of the past two days, he wouldn't have been surprised if Henrick and the Viking had been magically transported into outer space, or maybe even whisked away on the back of a giant hedgehog. Jimmy didn't remember ever being so frustrated. He was cold, wet, and exhausted.

"This is just great!" William said. "What do we do now?"

No sooner were the words out of William's mouth than the ground below the tree began to rumble.

"What's that?" Jimmy asked.

The three children exchanged a worried glance. Then a hole opened in the snow, and they were suddenly slipping.

SIXTEEN

The Underground Bunker

THE NEXT THING JIMMY KNEW, HE WAS CAREENING down a slick slide on his stomach. He then whooshed around a curve and rolled onto his back. Struggling to sit up, he shot out across a bright room into a padded wall.

Thump!

William and Janice were right behind.

Thump! Thump!

As Jimmy untangled himself from his friends, he saw that he had landed in a small underground laboratory. Henrick and the Viking were standing in front of a wall of computers. Though the room was warm, Henrick still wore his red earmuffs and the Viking his purple helmet and blue cloak. Rough pencil sketches of pods, wood-chucks, and spaceships were tacked to a bulletin board that hung above the computers. The far wall was covered in its entirety by a giant map of outer space. Nearby was a pile of used boxes—each one bearing the same logo as on the Sugarton space barge: PLASTAWOOD.

Despite his predicament Jimmy took hope from his surroundings. With proof that Henrick was connected to the woodchucks, maybe he could finally get some information about his father. But as he and his friends struggled to their feet, he heard a click. Before he could react, metal bars dropped from the ceiling, enclosing them in a small cell.

"Welcome!" Henrick cried before the trapped children could so much as cry out. His voice was surprisingly high and musical. "Allow me to introduce my friend and colleague, Genghis O'Leary, a direct descendant of the famous Viking Erik the Mauve. Or was it Erik the Red? No matter! We're both so pleased to see you! So good of you to slide in! Take off your wet coats and shoes and socks. This room is quite temperate! We'll throw them in the dryer for you. We like our guests to be comfortable! Don't we, Genghis?"

The Viking grunted. "I'm not much for creature comforts!" he said. His voice seemed to rumble out of him, so low and resonant it echoed off the walls. "Throw me on a bed of sharp spikes and I'll sleep just fine if I'm tired enough!"

Henrick giggled. "Ignore my friend. You know how

grumpy Vikings can get. Comes from wearing those heavy helmets. Or maybe it's because they lost North America to the Indians. But I digress! Allow me to formally introduce myself—to the boys, that is!" He bowed low. "Henrick Gustav Claytooth!" He stood back up. "I'm an inventor by trade. On Earth I'm known for my mute buttons. But in the universe? I've accomplished so much more! Why, there's the rocket-propelled fleet of automobiles I built for the third moon of Centurion. And the forty-thousand-mile suspension bridge currently under construction between the two moons of Plantangant! And my Viking friend adores my nuclear-powered roller skates. They're all the rage on the dark side of Venus!"

With that Genghis and Henrick began to pull food out of a small refrigerator near the wall of computers. "Now, who's hungry?" he said. "We have eggs. Sunny-side up or scrambled? Bacon, too. You kids must be famished after all that running around."

Jimmy had a sinking feeling in his stomach.

Henrick placed a carton of eggs on a small counter. Jimmy noticed a two-burner stove.

Henrick smiled, revealing a perfect row of teeth. Jimmy instantly thought of Angelina. But Henrick was finally looking toward his other daughter.

"How are you, dear? I'm so sorry about this little cage, but it's a necessity."

Janice was furious. It was one thing to be ignored on a daily basis. It was quite another to be caged.

"If you feel so sorry," she said, "then let us out of here!"

Henrick wheeled around to face the Viking. "Genghis, three hot chocolates for our guests! They're cold."

Genghis grunted again. "Have them ride through a blizzard on the back of a frostbitten woodchuck," he muttered into his thick beard. "Have them joust a mastodon with a ten-foot icicle! Then we'll talk about cold!"

"The hot chocolate, Genghis!" Henrick repeated.

"Save the breakfast," Janice snapped.

Henrick wheeled around, surprised.

"No breakfast? Aren't you hungry?"

Janice leaned into the bars, letting her anger build. For years she had dreamed of telling her father off, but she had never worked up the nerve. Now that she knew he was a main player in a plot to destroy the universe, she was all business.

"Let me make myself clear, Dad," she said. "You're going to let us out of here, and you're going to do it now!"

Henrick blinked.

"I am?" he said.

"Yes, you are!" Janice said. "YOU CAN'T JUST LOCK UP YOUR OWN DAUGHTER!"

"I can't?" Henrick looked suddenly uncomfortable. "Well, it is a tad unusual, I admit."

"Unusual?" Janice said. "It's horrible! So is lying! Boy, am I a fool! I can't believe I thought that you were out every night singing Gilbert and Sullivan when you were really out making giant killer woodchucks! You know what, Dad? That was time you should have been spending with *me*!"

Jimmy and William were flabbergasted. They had never heard someone speak so bluntly to a parent. In return, both boys fully expected that Henrick would be furious. In truth, Janice's words had the opposite effect. By the end of her short tirade Henrick was patting his pockets for a handkerchief. Not finding one, he dabbed his eyes with the Viking's thick beard, then blew his nose in his earmuffs.

"You're right," he said, leaning against the stove. "I told Genghis, just there in the woods, didn't I, Genghis? I said, 'I can't lock up my own daughter! It's probably not even legal in some states!'"

"It's not," Jimmy said. "Neither is kidnapping my father!"

Henrick blinked. "Your father?"

"One of your chucks snatched him," William said.

"But guess what!" Janice said. "You can begin to make it up to all of us."

Henrick looked truly happy. "Really? How?"

"By letting us out of here! Now!"

Jimmy expected Henrick to refuse. But to the boy's amazement, he reached into his pocket and pulled out a small silver key.

"Well, I suppose it's no harm. You won't get away with Genghis watching anyway. And I do hope you'll reconsider about breakfast! The eggs and bacon will be ready in a jiffy!"

Jimmy exhaled, heart pounding with relief. He knew that Henrick had only promised to let them out of the small pen, nothing more. But who knew what Janice would be able to convince him to do next? Seconds later Henrick had the key in the lock and the door open. But just as Jimmy was following Janice into the main room, a shrill voice pierced the air.

"What in the world are you doing? I told you to keep them locked up!"

Jimmy and William froze. They had met her only twice, but they knew exactly who it was. Janice was even more surprised.

"Angelina?" she stammered.

Just like the day before, Angelina was dressed for the riding ring, only this time her boots came up to her thighs.

Her hair was in a tight bun. She twirled a small riding crop in her right hand and smiled, showing every inch of her perfectly straight teeth.

"Surprised, little sister?"

Before Janice could respond, Angelina pushed her back into the cell, taking Jimmy and William along for the ride. Then Angelina slammed the door shut, sending the key jangling to the floor.

Rising to her feet, Janice shook the door, then looked at her father. "*Dad!* What's going on?"

Henrick giggled nervously.

"Come now," he said to Angelina. "There's no harm in letting them out. Not with Genghis here."

Angelina's wrist snapped forward. A sharp *crack* filled the room. As Henrick pulled away his hand, Jimmy realized what had happened. Angelina had whipped her own father with her riding crop! Again Jimmy expected Henrick to be angry. Instead, he rubbed his hand and glanced at Janice, obviously embarrassed.

"I'd love to help," he said. "But as you can see, I'm not the mastermind behind the giant frozen woodchucks." He shrugged. "Angelina is!"

"You?" William said.

Angelina grinned. "That's right, tubby."

Janice was stunned. "But you can barely do your math homework!" she sputtered. "I've written every book report you've ever been assigned!"

Angelina smiled. "I may not be book smart, sister, but I've got other skills."

"Angelina is a born leader," Henrick said. "Of course, I'm the one who invented the woodchucks—about two years ago on the mother ship—but it was Angelina who broke into my desk one night, looked at all of my drawings, and realized how everything could work together! She unleashed my potential!"

With that Henrick gave his daughter a kiss on the cheek. Angelina pushed him away.

"Dad!" she said. "Chill!"

Henrick giggled again. "So sensitive now that she's fourteen."

Janice still couldn't fathom what was happening. It was bad enough that her father was involved with the woodchucks. But her *sister*?

"What's going on?" Janice looked at Henrick. "What are you up to, anyway?"

Angelina met her sister's look with a smile so broad, her perfect teeth seemed to send shafts of lightning shooting around the room.

"Tell them, Daddy."

"It happened like this," he began. "One day in my laboratory something came to me quite by accident."

"Plastawood?" Jimmy asked.

"Exactly!" Henrick cried. "Plastawood! The first wood substitute in the universe! A plastic fiber that looks like wood and smells like wood but isn't wood!"

"Like the fake trees we saw on Sugarton," William said.

"Right again!" Henrick was warming to his story now, bouncing around the room like an excited elf.

Suddenly Jimmy got it.

"So you decided to have your woodchucks chomp everyone's trees so you could sell them Plastawood replacements!"

Henrick applauded. "Another score for the skinny boy! You get an A plus! But *I* didn't decide to sell the Plastawood. Angelina did! It was her pet project, you see. And it's working brilliantly so far. We've made a fortune on ten planets."

"You're crazy!" Janice said.

"And a murderer!" William said.

"Oh, no!" Angelina said. "Not murderers!" She smiled broadly. "Businesspeople!"

"Righto!" Henrick said. "We're very fair, aren't we,

Angelina? First we offer the planet the opportunity to pay us money up front. Only if they refuse—and can I help it if they all have so far?—do we send down the woodchucks. After that we find they're all too willing to pay for my Plastawood! And it really is lovely! Show them, Genghis!"

The Viking reached behind the stove and flipped a switch. The room dimmed as the map of the galaxy rose into a ceiling container revealing an image of a lush green forest.

"This is from Augustan in the Orion System," Henrick said. "Before my woodchucks arrived."

Henrick nodded and the slide changed. It was a shot of another forest, one that looked largely the same.

"And this is my forest of Plastawood! Beautiful, isn't it? And so much easier than the real thing! Tired of waiting for your tree to sprout? Well, Plastawood trees come fully grown, give off twenty percent more shade than a living tree, have a built-in beetle repellent, and never contract bark rot!"

"You're sick!" Jimmy said.

Angelina laughed. "No, we're rich!"

"But we're already rich," Janice said. "Thanks to mute buttons."

"Not rich enough," Angelina said.

Janice scowled. "I always knew you were a spoiled

brat. But how can you do this?"

Angelina smiled. "Because it's fun!" She turned to Genghis. "Is it scheduled to get warm in the next day or two?"

Genghis punched some numbers into a computer.

"Yes, miss."

"And the snow?"

"It should begin to melt tomorrow."

"Good!" Angelina faced her father. "Conditions for pod-to-chuck conversion are ideal. We'll shoot the pods to Earth from the mother ship."

Henrick waved his arms.

"Wait a second, sweetheart. Shouldn't we give the planet a chance to pay our fee before we destroy all the wood? That's what we usually do."

"Usually," Angelina said. She headed for a door on the far wall. "But not this time."

"But wait, darling," Henrick said. "What should we do with your sister and her friends?"

"Just what we planned," Angelina said. "We leave them here until the woodchucks come. They'll be safe underground and unable to interfere! Let's get moving! Genghis!"

Angelina stormed out of the room. As Genghis followed, Henrick plated the eggs and bacon and approached the cage.

"So sorry we can't take you to the mother ship. Some other time! Here are your eggs and bacon. Usually I like to add kumquat seeds. They're superb for night vision! Ah, well! Next time. But this food ought to hold you for a day or two. We'll be back once the planet is destroyed and we start rebuilding with Plastawood. Won't that be fun?"

Angelina's voice boomed from out the back door. "Daddy!"

"Yes, coming, dear!" He turned to the caged children a final time. "Eat! Eat!"

Then he scurried out of the room without a backward glance.

SEVENTEEN

A Surprise Passenger

WHEN JANICE WAS SURE ANGELINA, HENRICK, AND Genghis were really gone, she lifted her foot. Underneath was Henrick's key. William was so surprised, he came close to spitting out a mouthful of eggs. Indeed, it was such good fortune that Jimmy almost thought it was a joke—until Janice picked it up and opened the cell door.

"My dad's incredibly absentminded," Janice said. "When the key dropped to the floor, I just put my foot over it and hoped he'd forget about it."

"He might have wanted to forget," Jimmy said. "He seemed pretty guilty about locking you up."

"You think?" Janice said.

"Absolutely," William said, though the word came out "Ab-go-fruit-ly" due to a mouthful of food.

Janice and Jimmy pushed through the cell door into

the room. William shoveled a final bite of eggs into his mouth, grabbed two pieces of bacon for the road, and followed behind.

The way out was easier than the way in. Through the back door was a stairway that led to the large oak in the Ramble. Retracing their steps, the three children were soon back to the park's main road. They tried to put together the final pieces of the puzzle as they walked uptown.

"Okay, based on what Angelina and Genghis O'Leary were saying about the weather, the pods have to arrive on a planet while it's cold," Jimmy said. "When it warms up, they hatch."

"And we all know what happens then," William said. "They rip through the trees like a gazillion chain saws."

"Which means," Janice said, "that we've got to stop the pods before they're shot down to Earth. Once they land, there's nothing we can do."

"So what are our choices?" William asked.

"Just one," Janice said. "Fly to the mother ship and stop the pods before they're launched. Let's move!"

With that, Janice began to run. Jimmy followed right behind. Though William did his best to keep up, he was soon feeling the effects of his four doughnuts and his egg-and-bacon breakfast. With his gut aching, he slowed to a jog, then a walk. By the time he reached Janice's brownstone, he was lumbering along like a wounded buffalo, holding his side. His two friends were waiting for him out front.

"Guess I'm not in quite the shape I used to be," he said sheepishly. He leaned on the gate outside Janice's house, panting heavily. "Should we go up?"

"Afraid not," Jimmy said.

Then William noticed. Janice was pacing—and she didn't look happy.

"What happened?"

"I can't believe it," Janice said, half to herself.

"Believe what?" William said, breathing hard.

Jimmy broke the news. "Angelina took *The Fifth Floor.* We walked up the stairs and there was nothing there."

Jimmy and Janice sat sadly on the brownstone steps.

"Don't tell me you guys have forgotten about my go-cart?" William said.

Jimmy and Janice groaned.

"Your go-cart?" Janice said.

"Right!" William said. "Come on. Time's a-wasting!"

"To do what?" Jimmy said. "Die? That thing nearly killed us."

"That was yesterday."

"Yeah?" Janice said. "How will today be any different?"

"You forget," William said to the girl. "I've read your book!"

Janice shook her head. "No offense, Mr. President, but *Light Speed and You* is geared toward Level Three vessels. I don't know if it'll help us get your go-cart into space."

William was undeterred. "Then we can fix it together."

Janice frowned. "Together?"

"Okay," William said. "You can do it and I'll watch."

Janice waved an arm. "Too difficult."

When William turned to him for support, Jimmy looked away.

"Boy," William said, "I didn't chalk you guys up as quitters!" He turned to Jimmy. "You still want to find your dad, right? And Janice? I know you want to get back at your sister! And we all want to save the world! What other choice do we have?"

For a moment Janice and Jimmy were silent. Finally, Janice ran back into the brownstone. She returned a few minutes later holding a foot-high stack of typed pages.

"What's that?" William asked.

"The draft of my second book," Janice said. "*A Girls' Guide to the Milky Way*. I'm going to need all the help I can get."

Uptown they retrieved William's contraption from the back of Emma's Tea. As William and Janice got to work revamping it on the sidewalk, Jimmy brought his mother up to date on what had happened when they'd followed Henrick.

William and Janice were on their backs under the cart's back wheels. A thin line of orange smoke wafted out from one of the many pipes that rose in strands of twisted spaghetti out of the machine's engine.

"Will this thing be able to make the trip?" Emma asked.

William slid out from under his vessel, covered in soot.

"No problem, Mrs. Weathers!"

Just then Janice popped up next to him. "Triple-pronged reflux hammer! Now!"

William scurried to his tool kit and passed it to Janice, who disappeared back under the cart.

"I go on ship!" Imogene cried. With her purple backpack already on her back, she was ready for action. "*My* turn!"

She hoisted herself over the side of the cart and fell headfirst into the driver's seat. To Jimmy's surprise, she took his Game Boy out of her backpack and began to fiddle with the joystick, effortlessly making one of the crash helmets float in a circle around the cart.

"Whoa!" William said. "Not bad!"

Janice slid out from under the cart. "Did you do that?"

"I go on ship!" Imogene repeated.

"Oh, no you don't!" Emma said, pulling her back out. "I haven't decided whether I'm even going to let Jimmy go!"

Though Jimmy had no great desire to try William's go-cart again, he wasn't going to let his mother make the decision for him.

"And what?" he said. "Let the pods come down to Earth? Let the woodchucks eat all our trees?"

His mother forced a smile. "Maybe you'll understand one day when you have kids," she said. "But I'd rather live on a planet where the trees were all made of Plastawood than risk losing you."

She punctuated her comment by rubbing her hand through Jimmy's hair and giving him a kiss on the cheek. Jimmy sighed. Moms could be so melodramatic. Before he could plead his case further, three customers entered the shop.

"We'll talk," Emma said. "Come on, Imogene!"

"I play with the boys!"

"Imogene!" her mother said. "Come!"

Imogene stuffed the Game Boy into her backpack and

allowed herself to be dragged back inside the shop.

"So?" Jimmy asked. "What do you think?"

Janice nodded after Imogene. "Your sister's Game Boy is incredible."

"No, not that," Jimmy said. "The go-cart."

"Oh, the go-cart!" Janice wiped the grease off her hands with a paper towel. "It's a piece of junk."

William frowned. "What?"

Janice smiled. "But it has potential."

William beamed. "That's more like it!"

The orange smoke floating out of one of the many exhaust pipes turned pink.

"Just tell me," Jimmy asked. "Is this piece of junk going to get us into space?"

"Of course it is!" William exclaimed, kicking one of the front tires. "We rejiggered the coil to the interior fuel tank, then added another four inches to the outer retro-rockets!"

Jimmy sighed. "Janice?"

The girl shrugged. "I've seen stranger things fly."

"See?" William said. "We're golden!"

"Oh, all right," Jimmy said. "Just let me say good-bye to my mom."

But with Jimmy's first step toward the shop, he heard a loud whirr. While Jimmy, William, and Janice were talking,

Imogene had turned around, toddled quickly out of the shop, and snuck into the cockpit of the go-cart. Then she'd started to flip switches. Without knowing it, she'd pressed down the throttle. As Jimmy turned to look, the go-cart was rolling up the sidewalk toward Central Park.

"Whee!" Imogene cried. "Look at me!"

"Hey!" Jimmy cried. "Wait!"

The three friends were off like a shot.

"Stop!" William cried.

Luckily, Imogene hadn't pressed the throttle down very far and the cart was moving relatively slowly up the sidewalk. Sprinting full out, Janice and the boys were able to reach the cart. William grabbed onto a side bar and flipped himself into the cockpit. A moment later Jimmy and Janice did the same. Then William grabbed the wheel in the nick of time—just before the cart almost ran down an old lady carrying a bag of groceries.

"Watch it, young man!"

"Sorry!" William called.

"Me faster!" Imogene said.

"No!" Jimmy said. "Slower!"

"Hit the brakes!" Janice called.

But William was too tangled to reach them. The only one with a hand on the throttle was a two-and-a-half-year-old girl. Moreover, she was realizing something she considered extremely interesting. When she inched the throttle forward, the cart went faster.

"I go!" she called. "I go!"

She rammed it halfway down. Suddenly the ship was rocketing down the sidewalk.

"Whoa!" Jimmy called.

A boy dove out of the way. Then a girl.

"We go!" Imogene cried.

Now a policeman ran for cover.

"No!" Jimmy called.

"Stop this thing!" Janice called.

"I'm trying!" William called.

But when he tried to twist his body so his feet could find the brakes, Imogene pressed the throttle all the way down. The surge of power caused William to slip. His knee got wedged under the dashboard and pushed up the take-off bar. They were airborne!

"Wheeeeeeee!" Imogene cried.

She pounded the dashboard joyfully, oblivious to the fact that they were headed right at a tree.

"Ahhh!" Janice cried. "Watch it!"

William managed to cut the wheel. The cart swerved, and William guided the cart in a circle, back down 100th

Street. Jimmy glanced down. There was his mother, standing in front of her store, frantically waving her arms.

"Stop this thing!" Jimmy cried.

"I can't!" William said. "She put it in blast-off mode!"

"Blast-off?" Janice said.

They were high above the Hudson River now. Suddenly
the top whirred and closed.

"Yes, blast-off!" William called. "Hold on!"

The cart stuttered in midair, just as it had the day
before. Then came the surge of orange flame from the
engine. Then *boom!* Up it went!

"I flying!" Imogene called.

The force of the blast flipped her into Jimmy's lap and
pushed Janice into the middle passenger seat. A second
later there was another boom, this one even louder. To
Jimmy's surprise, the blue sky turned dark, then filled with
stars. Just like that, the four children were in outer space.
Maniacally working the controls, William took a second to
glance at Janice.

"We did it!"

Janice nodded, now smiling broadly. "Good job!"

Jimmy saw the faint glimmer of another blush light his
friend's face. In the course of a single day Janice had transformed from class geek to the person on the planet whose

opinion William most valued. For her part Janice had obviously warmed up to the chubby kid who shared her enthusiasm for space travel.

"Fly on, Mr. President!" she said, but now the nickname was affectionate.

William laughed, then pressed a button on his console.

"Roger that! Firing up the astral DNA analyzer!"

As a small compartment slid out of the dashboard, he reached under his seat and pulled out a dirty sweat sock.

"Oh, God!" Jimmy said. "Do you still have that?"

Imogene grabbed the sock, held it to her nose, and took a big whiff. "Daddy's sock!"

William took it from Imogene and dropped it back into the compartment, which then slid back into the dashboard.

"An astral DNA analyzer?" Janice asked.

"Now we can track Jimmy's dad to the mother ship," William said proudly.

"Yeah," Jimmy said. "If he's there."

"I bet he is," Janice said. "And if he isn't, I know some people on a space station in the Gingerbread Quadrant who should be able to help us locate the mother ship."

"Gingerbread Quadrant?" Jimmy asked.

"Of course!" Janice said. "Nine planets populated entirely by gingerbread men."

"Works for me!" William said.

"To Daddy!" Imogene cried. "To mommy ship!

With that William nudged the go-cart into light speed. Off they flew into deep outer space—two boys and two girls, guided by their faith in one another, their desire to save the planet, and a dirty sweat sock.

EIGHTEEN

The Mother Ship

IMOGENE TOOK OFF HER BACKPACK AND LEANED AS FAR forward in Jimmy's lap as she could, pressing her face up against the window.

"Look!" she cried. "Pretty stars!"

Jimmy wished that he could share in his sister's excitement, but once they were on their way, he found that he just couldn't get comfortable with the fact that William's rocket had once been nothing more than a simple go-cart, barely capable of hitting thirty miles per hour. Even with Janice's help, what were the odds that such a contraption could survive a journey through the galaxies? As they thundered farther and farther from Earth, Jimmy's mind spun with doomsday scenarios. They would be blasted to bits by a meteor, or burned to a crisp by the sun's gamma rays. Maybe run out of gas and get sucked into a black hole. No doubt about it: Sooner rather than later they would all be dead. Jimmy even imagined his poor mother weeping at his funeral.

Strangely, it was as he was picturing himself lying in a coffin that Jimmy began to cheer up. His thinking went like this: If the odds were strong that he was going to die anyway, why not just sit back and enjoy the flight while he could? How many boys got a chance to fly through space?

"Hey, look!" He pointed at a bright star to their left. "I think that's part of the Big Dipper!"

"Big Dipper?" Imogene asked.

"Just think of it as this giant ice cream scoop in the sky," Janice said.

Imogene's eyes lit up. "Ice cream? Chocolate?"

Jimmy looked at Janice and laughed. "Right. Chocolate."

Suddenly the ride was fun.

"Doughnuts!" Imogene cried, pointing to an empty City Donut bag lying on the floor of the cockpit. She riffled through her backpack, produced her Game Boy, and stood on Jimmy's legs.

"I point!" she cried, and pointed the toy at the bag.

"I click!" she went on, and held down a black button on the bottom of the toy. "I move!"

With that Imogene moved the directional stick toward her, and the bag rose into the air.

"Too cool!" William said.

As Imogene moved the stick in a circle, the bag circled too. Then, following a quick flick of her wrist, it slapped against the side of William's face.

"Good one, Genie."

The girl giggled, then accepted a high five from her brother.

"That teaches me to eat all the doughnuts," William muttered, crumpling the bag into a ball.

"Nice," Janice said to the girl. "I didn't even construct my first magnetized solar heat laser until my third birthday."

"How'd you do that, anyway?" William asked Imogene.

The girl shrugged. "I just fix!"

"See?" Jimmy said. "Simple!"

Imogene beamed. As she put the Game Boy back into her bag, Jimmy noticed something. A light on the dashboard had begun to blink green.

"What's that?" Jimmy asked.

"Hmmm," William said. "Your dad's sock is doing its work."

Janice blinked. "You mean he's that close?"

"According to my astral analyzer he is. If he's on the

mother ship, we should be getting there soon."

"We see Daddy?" Imogene asked.

"Looks that way," Jimmy replied.

Still, he was nervous. He hadn't expected the mother ship to be so close. Which meant that it might already be in range to release the woodchuck pods down to Earth. They had to hurry.

"Can't this thing go any faster?" Jimmy asked.

Imogene liked that idea. She reached across Janice and socked William on the shoulder.

"Go faster!"

"Genie!" Jimmy said. "That's rude."

Imogene frowned.

"We in space!"

"True," Jimmy said. "But you still have to be polite."

As William and Janice laughed, Jimmy made a mental note to relay the conversation to his mother when he got home. Even so, he wasn't stupid enough to think that the fact that he had kept after his little sister's manners while in outer space would do much to put his mother in a better mood. No doubt about it: If they managed to get home alive, she was going to be furious.

"Hey," he said to William. "Is there any way we can send a message to Earth?"

William shook his head. "No radio. No phone. No e-mail."

Jimmy was surprised. "You mean to tell me that you were able to build a rocket out of a go-cart, but you didn't think to include a communicator?"

William shot his friend an angry glance. "First things first, my man," he said. Then his face softened. "To tell the truth, I never really thought I'd get this thing into space."

Jimmy nodded. It was a fair point.

"Look!" Imogene cried.

A shooting star rocketed across the galaxy and disappeared, leaving a trail of bright orange. Imogene looked at Jimmy with a gigantic smile, then threw her arms around him.

"So pretty!"

"Yeah," Jimmy said. "It is."

Again he let himself forget that he was on a nearly impossible mission to save the planet. While William handled the controls, Janice, Jimmy, and Imogene pointed at stars, planets, and, once, a thunderous meteor shower. All the while, the small green light on the dashboard grew brighter and brighter. Finally William pointed.

"I think that's it," he said.

Jimmy peered ahead into space but saw nothing special—

only more stars, miles and miles of them.

"What?" he said.

"A little bit to the left and up," William said. "See it?"

Jimmy squinted. For a moment nothing. Then all of a sudden it was there—a gray dot.

"Bull's-eye!" Janice said.

"I see Daddy!" Imogene said.

Jimmy gave his sister a squeeze, and William pushed back the throttle. With a whoosh of purple smoke, the cart dove forward. As they drew closer, the small gray dot turned into an absolutely enormous five-sided silver ship spinning in space. Underneath each side was a giant exhaust pipe. Bright lights, the colors of the rainbow, shone from its top. Its sides were lined with rows of windows. Then a docking bay opened. Out flew a smaller, sleeker ship. Seconds later it had disappeared into space with a plume of fire.

"That must be where they land," Jimmy said.

"Right," Janice said. "And that's our way in."

"Won't someone see us?" William asked.

"Maybe," Janice said. "But unless you have some space suits in here, it's our only chance."

"Look!" Imogene said. "Ship!"

"Yes, we saw it, Genie."

"No! Two ships!"

Suddenly a new ship appeared near the docking bay. Unlike the sleek silver ship, it was a brown rectangle with no windows—another space barge!

"Exactly like the one we saw on Sugarton," Jimmy said.

"Stay away from it," Janice said. "A single cannon shot would blow us into the next galaxy."

"Don't worry," William said. "I'm going to follow it in!"

"Just don't let them see you," Jimmy said.

William narrowed his eyes. "Not with William H. Taft the Fifth at the controls!"

The boy inched the throttle forward and nudged the steering wheel. He soon brought his go-cart in line directly behind the large space barge. As the barge belched a stream of orange smoke from its exhaust pipes and moved forward, William finessed the go-cart controls and stayed right on its tail. Then he cut the throttle altogether. Jimmy could feel the ship begin to float forward on its own momentum. As the barge docked, the go-cart stayed tucked in its shadow and touched down behind it.

Imogene applauded. "We in big ship!"

William was all smiles. "Come on. Let's get out of this thing."

William undid a latch, and the top opened with a bright hiss of steam. Steel girders and metal pipes ran across the walls and ceiling.

"Looks like we're in a giant garage," Jimmy said.

Seat belt off, he lifted Imogene and placed her on the floor.

"Backpack!" she said.

"Shhh!" Jimmy said, and helped her on with it as William and Janice got out of the cart. Then William pressed a button and the top closed again. By that point Jimmy was very anxious to get moving. In every sci-fi movie he had ever seen, intruders were always greeted by a swarm of foot soldiers with laser guns. But William's landing had been even better than either boy could have imagined. It seemed they hadn't been noticed! Still, just as they were about to move away from their cart to investigate, there was the creak of an opening door. The children froze. Seconds later they heard footsteps and muffled voices—pilots leaving the barge. Then another door opened and shut, and the voices were gone.

"Close call," William said.

"Yeah," Jimmy said.

"So what next?" Janice asked.

"We go!" Imogene said.

Like most little children, she spoke at one volume: loud.

"Shhh!" Jimmy said. He got down on one knee. "We have to be quiet here, Genie."

"But I don't want to be quiet!"

The typical toddler answer. Jimmy gave her a hug.

"Just try, okay?" He then quoted his mother. "Use your little voice, all right?"

Imogene nodded but then replied at full volume, "My little voice!"

Jimmy looked at William and Janice. "We'd better cruise. Let's head out the door and look around the ship for signs of my dad."

William went first. Looking both ways to make absolutely sure that no one was around, he crept along the side of the barge. Janice went second, while Jimmy took up the rear, holding Imogene's hand. At the edge of the barge, William saw that the exit was on the far end of the room. The only way to reach it was to travel across a good forty feet of open ground.

"We'll be spotted if they've got a security camera in here," William said.

Jimmy stretched his arms out. "Come here, Genie. We have to move fast now."

He never would have guessed that carrying her to and from the park all those times would be training for something so important.

"Okay," Jimmy said. "Ready?"

"Ready!" Imogene said.

"Move it!" Janice said. She nudged William. "And really run this time!"

He did. By the time Jimmy reached the door, William was already pushing it open. Suddenly the children found themselves in a silent white corridor that went straight for fifteen feet before veering to the right.

"What now?" William asked.

There were no maps, no floor plans—no clues at all about where they were on the ship, not to mention the location of Jimmy's father or the pods. Jimmy sighed, at a momentary loss. Part of him wanted to cry out in a voice louder than Imogene's, "Hey, Dad! We're here! We're here!" But he kept his mouth shut. After all, the last thing he wanted was for Angelina, Henrick, and Genghis O'Leary to know that they were aboard—if they didn't already.

"We go straight, I guess," he said.

It wasn't long before Jimmy felt like a lab rat in some sort of strange psychology experiment. He and his friends were soon running blind down a series of corridors, all white, all separated by sliding doors. Right, then left, then up, then down. The children had no idea where they were going.

On the fifth hallway (or was it the sixth?), Jimmy tried to put Imogene on the ground.

"Hold my hand," he said.

"No, no!" Imogene said. "You carry me!"

Jimmy knew better than to argue.

"Here," Janice said, coming up to Jimmy's side. "I've got her."

She scooped Imogene into her arms, and on they went, down another hallway and then another. When Janice got tired, she handed Imogene to William.

"Are you really sure this is the right ship?" Jimmy asked finally.

William frowned. "What other ship could it be?"

Imogene squirmed back into her brother's arms.

"Who knows?" Jimmy said. He was becoming exasperated. "Maybe your astral DNA analyzer is wrong! Maybe we're on some other mother ship!"

William shook his head. "Out of the question."

Of course Jimmy knew his friend was right. This had to be the right ship. But that didn't make it any less frustrating. Were they close? Were they being set up?

"I know, I know," Jimmy said. "But where are all the people?" Imogene began to struggle out of his arms. "Genie! Chill!"

But Imogene pushed her brother in the chest, dropped to the floor, and began to run. Then Jimmy saw why. Down the hall a door swung open, filling the hall with a bright shaft of light. Coming from within was the murmur of voices and the low hum of machinery. The boys exchanged a glance and then sprinted down the hallway. The girls followed.

"Look!" Imogene said at the door. "People!"

It was true. Around the corner was the main control room for the ship. Workers, all in flowing robes and Viking helmets, staffed computer terminals. Funnels stretched down from the ceiling shooting steam and water into a series of pipes that then shot more smoke and water into other pipes. Most striking was the giant machine in the corner. Standing ten feet high and eight across, its front was filled with rows of switches and knobs. From out of its top rose two small smokestacks.

"Well, well, well! Look who made it after all!" Just like that Henrick was striding toward them. He had changed earmuffs—this time to a fluffy bright blue. "You know, I was half hoping you'd come. Look, dear," he called across the room to where Angelina sat behind a computer monitor. "Your sister is here!"

Angelina spun around in her swivel chair to face the new arrivals.

"You took my ship!" Janice called.

"Borrowed," Angelina said. "You never were very good at sharing your things."

With that she snapped her fingers. Genghis O'Leary grabbed Jimmy and Imogene; another Viking, this one with a black beard and an orange helmet, took Janice in his arms. A third Viking put William in a bear hug. Without missing a beat, Angelina turned to her father.

"We're ready!"

Henrick rubbed his hands together excitedly.

"You're just in time!" he told Janice.

"In time for what?"

Angelina smiled. "Think, sister dear! To watch us launch the pods!"

NINETEEN

The Podderizer

THAT WAS HENRICK'S CUE. HE HOPPED FORWARD, frantically rubbing his hands together.

"Yes, yes, yes! How exciting! How perfectly thrilling!" He turned to Jimmy. "Our first attempt to shoot pods to Earth was a complete failure. Due to a malfunction in our pod cannon, the only hit was the pod that grew into the woodchuck that your father and sister discovered!"

"So you did know about my father!" Jimmy said.

"Of course!" Henrick replied. "That's why we had to kidnap him—to make sure he wouldn't spread the word about the woodchucks before we could make a second attempt. But now that we've fixed the pod cannon, we can shower Central Park with enough pods to destroy the city in hours!"

"But where is he?" Jimmy asked. "You don't need to

hold him now that you're launching the pods!"

"Hmmm," Henrick said. "That's true enough."

"So you'll take me to him?" Jimmy asked hopefully.

Angelina had heard enough.

"Not a chance!" she said. "Prepare the pods!"

With that she cracked her riding crop against a desk a few inches from where her father was standing. Henrick jumped.

"I'm on it!" he said.

Deeply disappointed, Jimmy watched him bustle across the room to the giant machine in the corner, where he rubbed its shiny metal with his open palms.

"Meet my woodchuck podderizer!" he cried. For a moment Jimmy almost thought he was going to kiss it. "Isn't it beautiful? Isn't it luscious! Isn't it divine!"

"*Dad!*" Janice called sharply. "Don't do this!"

Henrick giggled. "Sorry, dear, but I can't help it! You know how I fall in love with my inventions! I still have dreams about my diesel-fueled mechanical lions! And don't get me started on my double-pronged three-story crater jumper! Anyway, time to get started! This is the easy part!"

Henrick snapped his fingers. Two Vikings grabbed him under his armpits and lifted him to the top of the machine.

"Here we go!" Henrick said with a giggle. "Get ready!"

With that he pressed a single gray button on the

machine's side, and the Vikings lowered him back to the floor. Though Jimmy still didn't know exactly what the machine was supposed to do, he did expect it to do *something*. But for the next few seconds it sat there, completely soundless, like a giant piece of useless metal. Out of the corner of his eye Jimmy even saw a few of the Vikings exchanging glances. Irritated, Angelina was drumming her fingers against her console.

"Fear not!" Henrick called, sensing the mood of the room. "It takes a moment to warm up!" He rubbed his cheek against the machine. "Don't you, my sweet baby?"

As if to answer, the giant machine suddenly belched a plume of white smoke. Then, somewhere deep inside, a gear turned with a faint creak.

"Yes! Yes!" Henrick cried, hopping from one foot to the other. "That's the spirit! There you go!"

Another gear turned, punctuated by a loud bang and a groan. Then a row of red lights around its side lit up, and the machine began to hum.

"Is it working yet?" Angelina asked. "I don't see any pods!"

"Patience, my dear!" Henrick called.

Whoosh! Flecks of ice sprayed out of the pipes on top.

Henrick all but skipped to the far side of the machine, rubbing his hands together.

"Now! Here it comes!"

As the podderizer belched a plume of yellow smoke, another round of ice burst out of its pipes. With a low whistle, a single pod suddenly appeared out of a hole in the side of the machine and rolled onto a moving conveyor belt. Jimmy gasped. The other pods he had seen had all been cracked open. But this one was a perfect oval, three feet long. More striking, it was covered with an intricate web of icicles!

"Yes! Yes!" Henrick shrieked. "Frozen pod number one!"

To Jimmy's surprise, the Vikings burst into a wild round of applause. Some stomped the floor with their boots. Janice and William looked horrified, but Angelina allowed herself a small, cunning smile. And now that the pod was out, it traveled on the conveyor belt all the way down the far side of the room over to the main control console, where it dropped into a round hole in the far wall.

"First pod loaded!" Henrick called.

"Excellent!" Angelina said.

"Pod!" Genghis O'Leary called.

The Vikings answered, "Pod! Pod!"

Jimmy shook himself. What a nightmare! There had to be a way to stop it. But how? Genghis was far too strong and was holding him far too tightly. Worse, now that it was warmed up, the podderizer appeared to be working well.

"Here come numbers two and three!" Henrick cried, all but dancing up the side of the machine. Jimmy looked just as two more icicle-encased pods rolled onto the conveyor belt. But that wasn't all. As the third pod dropped into the loading hole at the main console, the podderizer coughed, then began to hum at a higher pitch. The gears inside began to chug more quickly, and small blocks of ice shot out of its sides, breaking into small pieces and skittering across the floor. And then? In the blink of an eye, the rate of pod production exploded. The Vikings counted each one.

"Four pods!"

"Five!"

"Six!"

Each more perfect than the last, encased in a beautiful web of ice.

"Ten pods!"

"Fifteen pods!"

"Twenty pods!"

Jimmy met his friends' eyes. How many were they going to use, anyway? Thirty? Forty? How many woodchucks would it take to destroy a single city? But the machine was showing no signs of stopping. If anything, it was humming more smoothly now, effortlessly shooting out pod after pod.

"Thirty pods!"

The Vikings stamped their boots on the floor. Some clapped their hands and banged their helmets.

"Forty!"

By that point Angelina was looking through a viewfinder.

"Earth is almost in range!" she said.

Jimmy began to panic—especially when Henrick flipped another switch and the giant contraption began to shake back and forth like a washing machine on its final spin cycle. A moment later the pods began to pour out of its side.

"Forty-five!"

"Fifty!"

"Sixty!"

Henrick hopped up and down. "Yes! Yes! Yes! Look at all my gorgeous pods! See how each one is a perfect oval? How each is encased in a beautiful web of ice! Did you know that each one is frozen at exactly twenty degrees? And that each contains a beautiful frozen woodchuck that will grow into a giant tree-killing machine?"

Jimmy was stunned. The sound of the Vikings stomping on the floor was deafening.

"Seventy!"

"Eighty!"

"Ninety!"

And then—just when Jimmy began to doubt whether it would ever stop—the machine coughed, spewed a wild plume of smoke, and shot out a mad flurry of ten final pods. With a final whoosh of ice and a loud gasp, the machine finally shut down.

"Good baby," Henrick said, patting its side again. "Such a nice machine! One hundred beautiful pods!"

"All aimed for New York?" Jimmy stammered.

"Every single one of them!" Henrick said.

For one moment Jimmy was almost glad that Genghis was holding him. He felt so sick, he almost fell over. How would the city ever survive the attack of one hundred killer woodchucks?

And then Angelina laughed and looked up from her viewfinder.

"Earth is in range!"

Now that the pods were loaded, she didn't intend to waste any more time. She wheeled around to face her father.

"Fire on my command!"

TWENTY

Countdown to a Chucking

"**T**EN!"

Jimmy gasped. Did he really only have ten seconds before the pods that would destroy New York were launched? They might even devastate a large part of the United States before they could be stopped! And where was his father? Was he really somewhere on the ship? Would he ever see him again?

Jimmy tried to break away from Genghis.

"Think you can get away from me?" the powerful Viking whispered, holding him fast in one arm while Imogene struggled in his other. "I'll squeeze your innards out of your ears."

Janice was having no better luck getting free from the dark-bearded Viking.

"Dad!" she called, thrashing her legs. "Don't!"

Henrick was now seated at the main control panel, looking into a monitor.

"Relax, dear!" he called. "Earth will look lovely redone in Plastawood—maybe even better!"

"Nine!" Angelina called.

Jimmy closed his eyes. Was this a dream? Was he trapped in one of his father's unpublished stories?

"I go!" Imogene called. "I go!"

Imogene tried to squirm free, but was only able to ruffle Genghis O'Leary's cape.

"Easy, girlie!" the Viking hissed.

"Eight!" Angelina called, then turned to her father. "Are we certain the pod cannon is correctly aligned?"

"Absolutely!" Henrick said, rubbing his hands together. "All one hundred pods will hit the park, then sit there until the warm weather comes!"

"Don't do this, Dad!" Janice called. "They'll destroy Earth!"

Busy at the controls, Henrick didn't respond.

Angelina laughed. "Give it up, little sister! Seven!"

With that she flicked a switch. A steel wall parted, revealing a giant window. Jimmy gasped. There was Earth—so close, he felt he could reach out and touch it.

"It looks so pretty from up here, doesn't it?" Angelina said.

"You're insane!" Jimmy said.

Angelina cracked her riding crop against a chair. "Six!"

That was when William made his move. *Bam!* He smashed his heel against his Viking's booted big toe, then broke for Henrick. But after no more than three or four steps, he was surrounded and then carried, squirming and biting, to the back of the room.

"Put me down! I'm William H. Taft the Fifth!"

Imogene decided to accompany William's speedy capture with music.

"A spoonful of sugar helps the medicine go down!"

Jimmy looked at his sister, wishing that he could be two and a half, so carefree that he could sing in face of the end of the world.

"Someone shut that kid up!" Angelina called. "Five!"

Genghis dutifully covered Imogene's mouth with one of his hands, but Imogene continued to belt it out through his fingers. Though Jimmy was tempted to tell his sister to be quiet too, he stopped himself. He suddenly remembered where he'd been the last time his sister had sung a song from *Mary Poppins*—safe in their home, watching Imogene fiddle with his broken Game Boy—the same Game Boy that was now in her backpack! Which is when Jimmy got an idea. It was a long shot, but he had to try. As

Imogene brought her song to a stirring finish—"In the most delightful way!"—Jimmy inched his hand around Genghis's broad back toward her backpack.

"New York State is in line," Henrick said.

He gripped the firing mechanism. Angelina turned to Janice.

"It pains you, doesn't it? Watching the man who always paid more attention to me ignore you again and do just what I want!"

Janice refused to be baited.

"You can stop this, Angelina!" she said. "It's not too late!"

Angelina waved her arms toward the window. Earth appeared even larger.

"Oh, yes it is!" she said. "There's your home planet! Seconds from its first chucking! Four!"

Carefully, Jimmy undid the backpack flap, reached inside, and found the Game Boy. It seemed insane to think that it could redirect the flight of one hundred flying pods. He knew that. But what other option did he have?

"Three!" Angelina called.

Bam! In the back of the room, William tried again. He smashed his foot against his guard's boot, then elbowed another in the stomach. The two Vikings didn't so much as grimace.

"Two!"

Henrick was all concentration, focusing on his monitor, lining up his shot. Nearby, Jimmy was just as focused, his finger poised on the Game Boy's joystick, ready to redirect the shots the minute they were fired.

"Central Park in line!" Henrick said.

"Excellent!" Angelina said. "One!"

"Dad!" Janice called.

"You stop!" Imogene yelled.

"My great-great-great-great-uncle was president of the United States!" William cried from the back of the room.

"I go pee!"

Jimmy looked disbelievingly at his sister. He couldn't imagine a worse time to ask to be taken to the bathroom.

"Hold it in," Jimmy told her.

"No," Imogene shouted. "I really go pee!"

Then Jimmy blinked. He had always known Imogene was smart, but this was beyond anything he had a right to expect. A quick look at her pants showed no wet stains. Was his sister really creating a diversion? Apparently so. Better still, it was working! A worried glance crossed Genghis's face.

"Pee?" he grunted.

Imogene smiled. "You take me to potty?"

Genghis scowled and dropped her on the floor. Without missing a beat, Imogene sidled up to the Viking holding Janice and sat down on his boot. He screamed, dropped Janice, and pushed Imogene to the floor. Free, Janice sprinted for her dad. At first Jimmy was tempted to shout "Stop!" After all, if the Game Boy worked, the pods would be redirected into deep outer space. But then he realized something. With all eyes on Imogene and Janice, he had the momentary freedom to aim the Game Boy directly at the giant window.

"Fire!" Angelina commanded.

Janice landed on her father's back just as he pulled the trigger. A flurry of one hundred pods shot into space at the same time. Jimmy pointed the Game Boy out the window and pressed the button just the way Imogene had shown them on the go-cart. Then he toggled the joystick around in a wide circle. Even as he was doing it, it seemed absurd. Had it come to this? Had his hope for saving Earth and rescuing his father come down to the invention of a two-and-a-half-year-old? Worse, Jimmy had no way of knowing whether it had worked or not. He thought he had locked onto all the pods. In fact, he was certain of it. But they had whooshed into space so quickly that they were out of sight. All he could do was to toggle the joystick in a circle away from

Earth—or better yet, if he kept toggling in a circle . . .

"Stop him!"

It was Angelina. Before he knew it, Jimmy was wrapped in one of Genghis's powerful arms and the Game Boy had dropped to the floor. Then the Viking took three giant steps and jerked Janice to her feet.

"The pods are launched!" Angelina cried.

In unison the Vikings tossed their helmets in the air, then stamped on the floor, chanting, "Pod! Pod! Pod! Pod!" Angelina picked up Jimmy's Game Boy and laughed.

"What?" she said. "You thought this little toy could affect the flight of my pods?"

Jimmy swallowed hard. He had thought it could. In fact he still hoped it had.

"And you!" Angelina said, leaning close to her sister. "When will you learn that Rockland girls always win?"

Despite everything, Janice stood her ground. "Don't get cocky. You haven't won yet!"

Angelina laughed. "In your dreams, little miss rabbit face! You'll never stop me!"

"Now, now, Angelina." Henrick giggled nervously. "No need to rub it in, is there?"

In response Angelina cracked her riding crop against a table.

"Take them!" she called.

The guards acted quickly, pushing Jimmy, Janice, William, and Imogene past Henrick toward the door.

"Move!" Genghis O'Leary said.

Janice looked at Jimmy.

"We were too late," she said.

But Jimmy wasn't willing to give up hope. Perhaps that final flick of the joystick had worked?

"You never know," he whispered. "Just wait."

Janice wrinkled her brow. "For what?"

Just then a thunderous boom shook the room. Smoke began to stream out of the controls. An alarm sounded.

"For that!" Jimmy called.

"We're under attack!" Angelina called.

Another explosion rocked the room, sending everyone flying to the floor.

"You did this with Imogene's Game Boy?" William called.

He was under a table, flat on his stomach.

"I think so!" Jimmy cried. "The pods are circling back to hit the ship!"

By that point the two-and-a-half-year-old was the only one in the room standing.

"Go!" she said, pulling her brother up by his shirt. "We find Daddy!"

TWENTY-ONE

Escape from the Mother Ship

A S USUAL, JIMMY KNEW IMOGENE WAS DEAD RIGHT. Now was the time. Find their father, then escape.

But how could they do it with the mother ship under attack? In any case, the first step was obvious: He had to stand up. But as Jimmy staggered to his feet, he saw Genghis struggling to get up too. There was only one thing to do. *Bam!* Out shot his leg. His foot connected with the soft part of the Viking's large stomach. With a loud *oof!* Genghis went down.

"Nice!" William said.

"Hurry!" Janice said.

But Angelina was too fast. Up on her feet, she dashed across the room and blocked Janice's escape.

"Think you can get away from me, little sister?"

Just like that, she grabbed Janice's arm and twisted it hard behind her back.

"Ow!" Janice cried.

Henrick gasped. "Easy does it, Angelina!"

But Angelina was not to be stopped. A hideous grin spread across her face. "You know, Janice," she said, twisting her arm even harder, "sometimes I wonder if it bothers you."

"What are you talking about?" Janice asked.

Angelina laughed. "Come on, don't pretend you don't see how much better life would've been for Daddy and me if *you* had fallen into the seal pond along with Mom!"

Henrick blinked, stunned. Had he been so hypnotized by Angelina's vision of a universe dominated by woodchucks and Plastawood that he had overlooked her true nature? Had he raised a monster?

"Wait a second," he said.

"Oh, come on, Daddy!" Angelina barked. "You know it's true! Janice just takes up space!"

Henrick's eyes went wide. "No, no," he said. "That's not right!"

"Back off, Angelina," Janice called. Teeth clenched, she refused to give up. "Don't make me hurt you!"

Angelina chortled hysterically. "Hurt me? No! This is where I hurt you!"

With that she pushed Janice's arm all the way up her back, forcing her to the floor. Henrick had finally seen enough. Lowering his head like a bull, he charged his older daughter.

"Angelina!" he cried. "STOP!"

By that point Janice had already taken matters into her own hands. Grimacing in pain, she clenched her free hand into a fist, then spun around and punched with all her might. A loud crack filled the room. Just like that, Janice was free and Angelina was sprawled on the ground, her hands over her mouth.

"My teeth!" she cried. "My teeth!"

Except the words came out "My teef! My teef!" because two of them were on the floor beside her.

"Good shot!" William said.

Henrick took a quick step to help Angelina but then stopped and looked sympathetically at Janice. For a split second it looked like he was going to hug her. Then another pod hit, shaking the ship so forcefully, it seemed it might break apart. Flames burst out of the control panels. Black smoke filtered out of the podderizer.

"We've got to run for it!" Jimmy said.

"To Daddy!" Imogene said.

"But we still don't know where he is!" William said.

Jimmy felt a light touch on his arm. It was Henrick, pointing toward the main exit. "This way!"

"What?" Jimmy said.

Henrick was looking at Janice again. With a quick smile, he scurried off through a plume of smoke.

Jimmy looked to Janice. "Should we?"

She nodded, smiling herself. "Yeah. I think we should."

"We go!" Imogene called.

Jimmy scooped his sister into his arms. With Janice and William close behind, they dashed out of the room and down the hall.

"This way!" Henrick called through the smoke and flames. "Hurry! They're sure to follow!"

Swish! A door opened. They ran down a hall, then turned down another. *Swish!* Henrick turned left, then right, then right again. Then just like that he stopped and pressed a button on the wall. Suddenly the children were heading down a new hall, this one painted black. *BOOM!* Another pod hit the ship. Again the children were thrown to the floor. A new series of alarms was triggered. But moments later the children were back on their feet, following Henrick down a flight of stairs. Jimmy was nervous. Was he really accepting help from the evil genius behind the podderizer? Worse, was the mother ship about to blow? Maybe. Then suddenly Henrick was jangling a set of keys by a large brass door.

"Is he here?" Jimmy asked.

He was still worried that Henrick was going to lock him and his friends into a cell so they'd be blown up with the ship. Henrick put the key in the lock and pushed open the door. Heart pounding, Jimmy peered into a dimly lit room. At first his eyes had trouble adjusting. But in seconds the figure sitting on the bed before him came into focus.

It was his father! Despite the fact that the room was filled with smoke, books were knocked off the shelves, and a desk chair was upside down in the middle of the floor, he was sitting calmly on his cot, writing.

"Daddy!"

Imogene squirmed out of her brother's arms and wrapped herself around her father's legs. Jimmy was close behind and was soon in his father's arms. Only then did Jimmy notice that his father was dressed in the same pajamas he had been wearing the night he had been dadnapped.

"Jimmy!" he cried. "Oh, Genie!"

The family hugged tightly, too happy to speak.

"We came as fast as we could," the boy said finally. "Are you all right?"

"Fine," Richard said. "How's Mom?"

"Worried but okay," Jimmy said.

Janice snapped her fingers. "Shhh!"

The room went quiet. Down the hall was the un-mistakable sound of footsteps, followed by the booming voice of Genghis O'Leary.

"I'll rip them from forecastle to aft, then have their innards for dessert!"

William gulped. "They're coming the way we came!"

"How do we get out of here?" Janice asked.

"Quick!" Henrick said. "The closets!"

"What?" Jimmy said.

The footsteps reverberated loudly down the narrow halls.

"I'll spike the lot of them on my helmet horns and make a tasty shish kebab!" Genghis cried.

Henrick was so excited, he ripped off his earmuffs. "Just hide!"

Jimmy, Janice, Richard, and Imogene scrunched into the closest closet. After trying to fit in with them, William crammed into one of his own and managed to close the door just as Genghis O'Leary stomped in the room. Through cracks in the closet doors, the children and Jimmy's dad could see that the red-bearded Viking had arrived with a squadron of at least ten other guards. Each man was bigger than the next. Each had a long, full beard and giant helmet. Most striking, each carried a whip.

Henrick pointed down an adjoining hall.

"I'm so glad you came, Genghis!" he said. "The kids took him that way! Hurry!"

Genghis snapped his whip. The crack was like a pistol shot. "You heard him! Move!"

In seconds the Vikings were hustling noisily down the hall. Genghis grunted thanks and stomped after his men. But he was just a step out the door when a loud, high-pitched sound came from one of the closets. Imogene had sneezed. The Viking stopped short and wrinkled his brow. Holding his whip high, he took a step back into the room.

"What in the name of Erik the Blue was that?"

"My stomach," Henrick said quickly. "It's been making the strangest grumblings all day. Must've been the pineapple I had you put in my eggs. Now go!"

Genghis took another step toward the closets. "I thought it came from in there."

"No, down the hall!" Henrick said. He paused. "You don't want me to have to tell Angelina that you let her sister get away, do you?"

Genghis nervously pulled at his beard. Listening from inside the closet, Jimmy was amazed how one fourteen-year-old girl had terrorized so many grown men.

"Of course not!" Genghis grunted.

"Then hurry!"

With that the Viking was following his men down the hall. A moment later the children spilled back into the room.

"I need Kleenex," Imogene said.

As Richard found his daughter a piece of tissue, Janice turned to her father.

"Wow, Dad," she said. "Thanks."

Henrick shook his head. "I've been a fool."

Janice paused. "A fool?"

Henrick nodded, his eyes glazed with a deep sadness. "Angelina had it all wrong. I never wished you had died along with Mom."

Janice bit her lip. "Yeah. I know that."

To the girl's surprise, her father reached out and touched her cheek. "You remind me of her so much." He closed his eyes for a moment. "What I'm trying to say is you were right. I was wrong to be spending so much time on woodchucks instead of with you."

Jimmy thought he saw the corners of Janice's eyes getting wet.

"There's still time," she managed. "I'm only ten."

Henrick smiled. "Yes! We do have time, don't we?"

"Why don't you fly back to Earth with us?" Jimmy asked. "We'll cram into the go-cart."

Henrick shook his head. "I've got to free the Grindlepickers on Sugarton and make things right on the other planets we destroyed," he said. He looked at Janice. "And then I have to talk some sense into your sister."

Henrick and Janice hesitated, not knowing what to do next. Then, just like that, they hugged—tight.

"Safe trip home," Henrick said.

Now a tear was rolling down Janice's cheek. "You too."

"You better get going," Henrick said.

"And fast!" William said. He turned from the door. "They're coming back!"

It was true! The heavy *clomp*, *clomp* of eleven Vikings in workboots was echoing in the hall. Henrick looked quickly out the door.

"They must've figured out I was lying! Run for your ship!"

Henrick gave Janice another hug. Then, to the children's surprise, he ran to the opposite side of Richard's cell and opened a trapdoor near the side wall.

"See you in space," he said, and threw himself headfirst down the shaft.

"Dad!" Janice called.

"He'll be all right!" Jimmy said. "We've got to go!"

They heard Genghis O'Leary's voice bellow down the hall.

"I'll turn each one of those no-good brats inside out, then right side in! I'll fillet them on a skillet with dog livers, then smear them with raspberry jelly!"

"Jelly! Jelly! Jelly!" the Vikings chanted.

"Move!" Jimmy called.

Richard scooped Imogene into his arms. Seconds later Jimmy was leading his crew back up the flight of stairs, now so smoky it was hard to see more than a few feet ahead and even harder to catch a decent breath. But on they ran—*Swish!*—through a sliding door, and suddenly they were back in the rat's maze, moving up, then down, then left, then right past smoke and fire. Still, no matter how fast they moved, they could hear Genghis and the Vikings hot on their trail. The *stomp, stomp* of their boots reminded Jimmy of the *thump, thump* of the woodchucks on Grindlepick. They were gaining fast!

"Hurry!" Jimmy cried.

They ran down the final hall and burst into the docking bay.

With *The Fifth Floor* still nowhere in sight, Jimmy led the way past the barge.

"To go-cart!" Imogene called just as Genghis and his men barreled through the door.

"Charge!" the Viking cried.

Giant whips slapped the floor. Richard and the children sprinted past the barge. William pressed a button on the go-cart's hood, and it opened with a loud hiss. Richard leaped into one of the passenger seats with Imogene in his lap, while Jimmy and Janice did their best to wedge themselves next to William at the controls.

"Careful!" William said. "I need to reach the throttle!"

"Sorry!" Janice said. "I can't move!"

Jimmy tried to make himself as thin as possible. Janice too. In the end she had one butt cheek on William's chair and Jimmy had one butt cheek on Richard's. Meanwhile Genghis and his squadron were seconds away.

"Kill!" the Viking called.

"Floor it!" Richard said.

William slammed on the throttle—but in the mad rush, he forgot to straighten the wheel. Instead of going forward, the go-cart wheeled around and barreled straight toward Genghis and his men! The big Viking and two others dove for cover; a fourth wasn't fast enough. The go-cart ran over his foot.

"Arrrgghh!" he cried.

"Turn!" Jimmy called.

William cut the steering wheel seconds before smashing into the barge. With a giant screech, the cart

fishtailed to face the right direction.

"Okay," William said. "Let's try that again!"

He pressed the throttle. This time Genghis was ready. As the cart thundered forward, he threw himself on the windshield. For a brief second William's view was completely blocked by the Viking's face, twisted in a horrible grimace.

"Swerve!" Janice called.

William cut the wheel back and forth. But Genghis held on tight. He then reached into his pocket and produced a giant axe.

"He's going to smash through the window!" Richard cried.

Genghis raised his arm high. But just as he was bringing it down, William cut the wheel again. Finally the Viking lost his grip and crashed onto the garage floor ten feet from the edge of the runway. With a giant whoosh the go-cart shot into space. Jimmy looked back over his shoulder to see Genghis crawling to the lip of the runway, clenching his fist.

"Look!" Imogene cried.

Jimmy blinked. He knew there had been multiple explosions, but he still didn't expect so much of the mother ship to be on fire. Flames burst out of windows and from the five giant exhaust pipes.

"Those pods really did some damage," William said.

"Did all one hundred pods hit the mother ship?" Janice asked.

"I think so," Jimmy said. "Or got shot into outer space."

Imogene glanced up at her father. "Earth okay?"

"Yes!" Richard said. "Earth okay."

Just then Jimmy pointed. "Look!"

A small ship whooshed into view from the other side of the flaming mother ship.

"Oh my gosh!" Janice said as it flew closer. "It's *The Fifth Floor*!"

A moment later the go-cart was by its side. Henrick waved through the front screen, then whooshed off to other parts of the universe.

"This is great!" Jimmy said. "Both our dads made it!"

The good news was punctuated by a positively enormous boom. Jimmy and crew looked to the mother ship: It was fully engulfed in flames now. A second later a light as bright as the sun filled the window. There was another boom—this one even louder—and the mother ship exploded. The little go-cart shook violently, but in seconds it was over. The mother ship was gone. Jimmy gulped. He looked at Janice.

"You okay?"

"Sure," Janice said. "Dad'll be fine in *The Fifth Floor*."

"Actually," Jimmy said, "I was thinking about your sister."

He nodded toward the spot in space where the mother ship used to be.

Janice swallowed. "Yeah, thanks for the thought," she said. "But knowing Angelina, she got off in time too."

For the next few moments the travelers rode in silence, out of respect to those people on the mother ship who didn't make it. Finally William saw a distant dot in space.

"Hey, look!" he called.

Richard, Imogene, Janice, and Jimmy looked up. There they were: the blues and greens and whites of Earth.

"Home," William said.

"It'll be good to be back," Richard said.

Jimmy nodded. "You can say that again!"

TWENTY-TWO

The Third Sighting?

WHEN HER SON AND DAUGHTER DISAPPEARED INTO space, Emma had no desire to be laughed out of the police station again. So instead of reporting what had happened, she simply cried, then brewed herself a cup of hot tea and returned to work. She was between customers, standing outside her shop in a sweater and winter coat, when William's go-cart touched down on 100th Street.

"Richard?" she said when the cart roof lifted open. "Is that really you?"

"Yes!" Jimmy's father said. "Back from space!"

While his parents ran into each other's arms, Jimmy got busy thinking up responses for the inevitable moment when his mother asked him to explain why he wasn't able to stop the cart from taking off with Imogene aboard. To his surprise Emma was so happy to have her family home, all she could say was "Let's celebrate!"

Soon the Weatherses and William and Janice were seated around a circular table at Pizzabella, a restaurant next door to the tea shop, for a late lunch of salad, spaghetti, and pizza. As they ate, everyone took turns filling Emma in on what had happened aboard the mother ship. Throughout, it seemed to Jimmy that his parents never took their eyes off each other.

"So?" his mother said. "What do the woodchuck slayers want to do this afternoon?"

"Hmmm," Richard said. "Shouldn't we send these kids to school for the last couple of periods?"

"Oh, man!" Janice said.

"Yeah, no way, Mr. W.," William said.

"Give us a break, Dad."

It seemed entirely unfair to make them go to school on the same day they had saved the world.

Richard smiled. "Just kidding. I think a day off is in order." He looked to William. "We'll find a way to explain it to your parents."

Then Emma cleared her throat and looked at her husband. Richard put an arm around Janice.

"You know, you're welcome to stay with us until your father gets back."

Janice smiled. For years she had been terribly lonely in her brownstone with only Angelina and Narice for company. But now that she had patched things up with her father, she was looking forward to getting home.

"Thanks," she said. "But I'll be okay with Narice. And my dad should be back soon."

"All right," Emma said. "But you come over anytime."

Janice nodded. "I will."

"So?" Jimmy asked. "How about a movie?"

There were a few he wanted to see. But before his parents had a chance to answer, Jimmy saw something odd. Outside, a man stopped in front of the restaurant window, staring overhead. He pointed up, then hurried off.

"That's weird," Jimmy thought.

Just then the quiet restaurant was filled with the sound of a piercing scream. A moment later a siren began to wail. Finally a woman with hair so frizzy she appeared to be plugged into an electric socket stopped by the restaurant window.

"Don't!" she cried. Like the man, she was also looking up. "Just don't!"

The boys and Janice exchanged a chilled glance.

"Are you thinking what I'm thinking?" William asked.

Jimmy and Janice nodded. Especially when another

woman stopped at the window, dropped to her knees, and screamed.

"But it's not warm enough for the pods to hatch," Janice said.

"Maybe they hatched anyway?" William said.

"Wait a second," Jimmy said. "I sent all those pods into space. At least I thought I did."

Then Janice remembered something.

"Don't forget! When my dad was firing, I rushed him and hit his hand!"

"But that couldn't have done anything," Emma said. She paused. "Could it?"

Before Janice could answer, another siren, this one even louder than the first, filled the restaurant. Suddenly a fire truck screeched to a halt outside the door. A moment after that, a police car pulled up. Through the window, Jimmy saw Officer Garcia get out. Then came Officer Lowe, stuffing what appeared to be an entire bagel into his mouth at once.

Jimmy's mother looked stricken. "I thought the mother ship exploded."

"It did, Mom," Jimmy said.

Then Imogene put into words what no one had said out loud.

"More woodchucks?"

Jimmy and his friends gulped. The image of what the enormous rodents had done to Grindlepick was all too clear in their minds, as was the terrifying *thump, thump, thump* of the horde that had chased them through the cotton candy fields.

For a moment Jimmy was overcome by a powerful urge to sprint out the back of the restaurant and run for his life. But no, he was in too deep to run. If there were woodchucks in the city, he had to help defeat them. Apparently the rest of his family and his two friends felt the same way. As if on cue, they rose to their feet as one and walked toward the door. Then Richard turned to his wife.

"Why don't you wait inside?"

Emma held up a hand.

"I don't want to be separated from you again," she replied, then forced a smile. "We're all in this together."

"Yes!" Imogene said. "We see the chucks!"

There was nothing more to be said. His heart beating like mad, Jimmy led the way to the restaurant door. How many woodchucks would there be? One? Two? Twenty? Were there any trees left in Central Park? In all of New York State? How many people had been trampled? Steeling himself for the worst, Jimmy stepped onto 100th Street. His family and William and Janice spilled out behind him. Together they looked toward Central Park.

"What?" Jimmy said. "Where—?"

He was too stunned to finish the thought. He had been certain that the horizon would be dominated by a team of gigantic woodchucks. But with the exception of the fire engine, police car, and a small crowd of onlookers, the street was practically empty.

"Have they run to the park?" William asked.

"Could be," Richard said.

"Kitty cat!" Imogene shouted.

Jimmy blinked. As usual, his little sister was right. Holding up a hand against the sun, Jimmy saw the cause of all the commotion. Perched on a thin ledge six flights up was a very nervous-looking black-and-white cat. The fire engine was raising its ladder to initiate a rescue. Richard was the first to laugh.

"Who ever said New Yorkers weren't kind?"

Emma nodded with relief. "I think it's going to take us a while to get over these woodchucks."

"Boy, you can say that again," Janice said.

Jimmy smiled. "It sure is."

Still, he felt disappointed. There was part of him that had been looking forward to a final showdown with the giant rodents. He didn't know how, of course, but he had seen himself as the savior of the planet. He even imagined himself on the front page of *The New York Times*:

Boy Hero Saves City from Four-Legged Terrorists!

Just then Officer Garcia caught his eye. She waved and strolled across the street.

"Hey there," she said. Then she turned to Richard. "Are you—?"

"Yes," Emma said. "My husband."

Officer Garcia nodded. "I'm glad."

Jimmy was about to blurt out everything—tell Officer Garcia all about Janice, their trip to Grindlepick and Sugarton, the underground bunker, Angelina, and the mother ship. But then he stopped. He knew she would never believe him.

Apparently Richard thought the same thing.

"Sorry to cause you alarm," he said. "I was out of town visiting a sick aunt and thought I had told my wife." He shook his head. "I'm pretty absentminded sometimes."

Garcia nodded. "That sort of thing happens all the time. Glad to have you home." She smiled again. "But I must say, your family has quite an imagination."

"Oh, that's my fault," Richard said. "I write kids' books."

Garcia smiled, then glanced overhead. "Looks like we have a kitten to save."

As she walked back to join Officer Lowe (now eating a slice of pizza), Jimmy frowned.

"What's wrong, son?" his father asked.

"I don't know," Jimmy said. "It just seems unfair that we did all that work and had such a wild adventure and we can't even tell anyone about it."

"Don't be so sure," Richard said. "There may be a way to get the story out."

Jimmy grinned. "I get it! You're going to make this your next book."

Richard raised a single eyebrow. "You're assuming I haven't already started!"

"What?" Emma said. "You mean you— When?"

"On the mother ship!" Janice said.

"You were writing when we found you!" William said. "Nice, Mr. W.!"

Richard shrugged. "I had to do something in my spare time, right?"

Then Jimmy remembered something. He reached into his back pocket and held out the piece of his father's draft he had been saving.

"Maybe this will help. I got it from a tree on 106th Street."

His father smiled. "Yes! Yes!" he said. "I was working on it the night I was snatched!"

"How's this for an opening sentence?" Jimmy asked. He cleared his throat. "'As Jimmy Weathers helped his mother set the table that Saturday evening in early April, he had no idea that the fate of mankind was about to come crashing down on his shoulders.'"

Richard wagged his head. "I like it!"

"Wait a second," Jimmy said. "I was kidding."

"No, it's good," Janice said.

"Right," Richard said. "Who's got a pen?"

Emma found one in her bag. A moment later Jimmy was repeating his opening as his father wrote it down.

"This one is going to sell, Mr. W.," William said when they were done. "I can feel it."

"Me too," Emma said, and gave her husband a kiss on the cheek.

"Big book!" Imogene said, but then quickly reminded everyone of the more immediate drama. "Look! Kitty!"

The ladder was raised now, and a young fireman was about to climb up. The group stayed to watch the successful rescue. When the cat was safely down, they cheered along with everyone else on the street.

"So?" Richard said. "How about that movie?"

He got no argument from the kids. Emma closed the shop for the rest of the afternoon. Though it was a good film—an adventure about a boy and girl who save the city from a killer tidal wave—halfway through, Jimmy and Janice noticed that William was hunched over, scribbling on a piece of yellow paper.

"What are you doing?" he asked.

William folded the paper. "Oh, nothing."

"No, what?" Janice asked.

William sighed then whispered. "On the way to the mother ship, I spotted the perfect planet."

Jimmy and Janice looked at him blankly.

"For Taftia!" William said, irritated. "I'm working on the constitution now."

With that there was a loud whoosh. On screen the giant tidal wave was picking up momentum, moments from flattening Boston. As Jimmy turned back to the movie, William reread what he had sketched out so far.

In the course of human events, when a people become dissatisfied with the social order of their home planet, they might band together to form a new civilization where the weak aren't excluded from recess and each meal is accompanied by dessert.

William looked back up at the screen. Though the tidal wave was thundering into downtown Boston, he didn't see a thing. Instead, he thought about the next clause of his constitution. When he had it clearly in his mind, he committed it to paper.

Let it be known that this planet will be ruled by a king, who may or may not be slightly overweight, as well as a beautiful queen. Let it also be known that if the aforementioned queen has very bucked teeth, it won't matter.

Now William smiled. He'd show it to Janice later. If he had the guts.

TWENTY-THREE

Recess

THE NEXT AFTERNOON SNOW PATCHES WERE TURNING to slush and the boys and girls of Class 5E were so sick of winter, they decided to pretend it was spring. After lunch Jimmy's entire class marched en masse to Central Park for the first kickball game of the season. Jimmy got an idea on the way over. At the park's edge he approached Tom Florie, the self-appointed ruler of everything athletic in the grade.

"Hey? Mind if I'm a captain today?"

Tom shrugged. "Why not?"

When they got to the field, students got busy digging snow off the baselines and chipping bits of ice off home plate while their teacher, Miss Espinoza, supervised.

"All right," Tom said after he deemed the field ready to play. "Let's choose up! Weathers goes first!"

As Jimmy looked them over, the class gathered in a clump by the backstop. His two friends stood on the outer edge of the group. While William was usually picked last, Janice usually wasn't picked at all. In fact, Jimmy couldn't remember the last recess period that she hadn't spent at her desk, reading a book. But to Jimmy's surprise, she had arrived at school that morning wearing a new pair of running shoes. And when she had smiled, he and William had nearly fallen over.

She was wearing braces!

"When in the world did that happen?" William asked.

Janice explained: "My dad got home late yesterday afternoon with *The Fifth Floor* to take me to the orthodontist before heading back to Sugarton." She smiled. "Goodbye, buckteeth!"

Jimmy couldn't have been happier. Still, he knew it would take more than the prospect of straight teeth and a new pair of sneakers to convince his classmates that Janice was cool.

"Pick, Weathers!" Tom Florie said. "Time's wasting."

Jimmy's heart was suddenly racing. While not the most popular boy in the grade, he definitely had the class's respect. What would his friends do when they discovered that he had become buddies with Janice Graygoof?

"Go ahead," William said, meeting Jimmy's eyes. He

nodded toward their new friend. "Pick!"

Jimmy knew that if he hesitated, he might change his mind.

"I've got Janice."

"Janice?" Tom Florie said. "You've got to be kidding."

The rest of the class was quick to put in their two cents.

"What's she going to do? Run the bases in a flying saucer?"

"No! She'll kick the ball with her fat front teeth!"

Though unoriginal and overused, these insults were considered hysterical by the class. Jimmy was embarrassed to realize that a week earlier he would have joined right in.

"Come on, Jimmy," Tom said, stepping forward. "Who's your first pick? For real."

Jimmy knew that he still had time to back out—to pretend that he was making yet another in a long line of jokes at Janice's expense. But how could he do that after all they had been through together?

"No, you heard me," he said. He looked at Janice. "Come on!"

This time the class was too stunned to say a word. As for Janice, she began her way to Jimmy's side slowly, lips tight. But by the time she reached him, she was smiling so wide, the metal from her new braces seemed to glint in the spring sun.

"Thanks."

"Just sprint like you did on Grindlepick and you'll do great," he whispered.

After the odd start, the class settled down. Tom took Allen Carpenter, another good athlete, and Jimmy took William. The rest of the group was divided quickly.

The game began. Though Jimmy was nervous the first time Janice came up to the plate, he soon realized that he didn't need to worry. Janice was a natural athlete who could kick almost as well as she could run through fields of cotton candy. In the last inning she booted the ball over the left fielder's head and found herself running for home to a sound she had never heard before in her life: kids cheering—for her!

"Slide!" Jimmy cried.

By that point the shortstop had the ball. He threw to Tom Florie, who was covering home. But Janice came in with such force that she knocked the ball clear out of the athlete's hands and sent him flying up in the air. A somersault later, he landed flat on his back.

"Safe!" Miss Espinoza called.

In seconds Janice was swamped. As his team mobbed his new friend, Jimmy couldn't help but think back to their first meeting two days earlier. It seemed ages ago that he and William had interrupted Janice as she contemplated drowning herself in her father's hot tub. Now Tom Florie gave her a grudging nod as he picked himself up from the slushy ground.

"Good game!" Miss Espinoza said. "Now back to school! Long division!"

As the class groaned, Jimmy picked up the kickball and joined Janice and William.

"Nice shot," he said.

William smiled. "You mean my slow roller to the pitcher?"

"Sorry," Jimmy said. "I was talking about our new superstar here."

"Oh, whatever." Janice smiled. "Tom really should have gotten out of my way."

Up ahead Miss Espinoza stopped the class at the edge of the park drive.

"We all cross at the same time, understood?"

"Sheesh," William said. "Who does she think we are? Infants?" He looked both ways. "There aren't even any cars coming."

"True," Jimmy said. "But you forgot about other modes of transportation."

"What?" the chubby boy said. "A spaceship?"

Jimmy blinked. "Try a . . . *dog*?"

With a glance up the bridle path, the three friends saw an absolutely enormous Saint Bernard coming closer at a brisk trot. Atop the animal's back was a teenage girl.

"A girl on a dog?" William said. "That's insane!"

Perhaps, but something about the rider caught Jimmy's eye. With a closer look he saw the tightly fitting riding boots and the arrogant smirk. His heart froze.

"Do you see what I see?" he asked Janice.

Janice nodded. "I told you she'd find a way off the mother ship."

William had noticed too.

"Holy Department of Missing Persons! It's Angelina!"

A moment later she drew her giant dog to a halt. She was riding bareback, and her ankles scraped against the ground.

"Angelina?" Janice said. "What in the world are you doing on a dog?"

Angelina blinked. "A dog?" she said. "This is Flicker, my horse!"

Janice, Jimmy, and William exchanged glances. Had the destruction of the mother ship and the foiling of her evil dreams turned Angelina mad? But there was more. Up close, Janice, Jimmy, and William saw that Angelina had

had dental work in the past day. In place of her missing teeth were two fake ones, slightly yellowed and too long for her mouth.

"This is too perfect!" William said. He smiled at Angelina. "How does it feel to look like a woodchuck?"

Angelina wasn't amused. "Shut up, fatty. These are temporary."

"Who put them in?" Jimmy asked. "Genghis O'Leary?"

Angelina's eyes narrowed. "As a matter of fact, yes—on our escape jet from the mother ship. I'm meeting him now to wait for the pods to hatch."

Jimmy blinked. "What?"

"Ignore her," Janice said. "She doesn't know what she's talking about." Janice turned to her sister. "I don't see how you can even show your face on Earth after what you've done. If Jimmy hadn't been so quick, the entire city would be overrun by killer woodchucks by now!"

By that point Tom Florie had sauntered over.

"Killer woodchucks?"

Suddenly everyone was dead quiet, waiting for an answer. Despite her recent triumph on the kickball field, the students of 5E were all too willing to demote Janice Graygoof back to the level of class weirdo. Jimmy wasn't about to let that happen.

"No, no," he said. "There are woodchucks in Janice's basement, that's all."

"Yeah," William said. "With big teeth and killer claws."

"Okay," Tom said. "But who's the crazy girl riding the dog?"

Angelina grinned. "Oh, I'm not crazy. Not a bit."

Miss Espinoza turned to Janice. "Is this girl your sister?"

Janice nodded as Angelina flashed a sudden smile and extended her hand. "You must be Janice's teacher. I've heard nothing but good things."

"Well, well," Miss Espinoza said. "Are you off from school today?"

"I go to Rockland," Angelina said haughtily. "Horseback riding is a graduation requirement."

Miss Espinoza was at a loss for words. As the class snickered behind her, she leaned close to Janice.

"Am I seeing things, or is your sister on a dog?"

Janice nodded. "That's right."

"Should we call your father?"

"My father?" Angelina cut in. "He's off trying to save Sugarton."

Miss Espinoza blinked. "What?"

Angelina turned to Janice, Jimmy, and William. "You guys can make fun of my teeth and my horse all you want, but the joke's going to be on you."

"What are you saying?" Jimmy asked.

Angelina smiled. "Oh, nothing. I just love the first warm breezes of spring right after a snowstorm, don't you?" She glanced back at Janice. "It's so satisfying to watch new things grow."

With that she gave her Saint Bernard a kick, and the dog broke into a quick trot. Jimmy, Janice, William, and the rest of the class watched her bump down the bridle path, ankles scraping the dirt.

"New things grow?" Jimmy said nervously.

"Relax," William whispered. "There aren't any pods on Earth."

"Yeah," Janice said. "They either hit the mother ship or went into space. Right, Jimmy?"

The boy didn't know what to say. How could he be sure that the Game Boy had redirected all one hundred pods? What if some of them had hit Earth after all? Worse, what if that was the reason Angelina had returned to the planet so soon? Yes, she seemed to be out of her mind, but maybe it was just an act? Maybe she was back to watch while the woodchucks had New York City for breakfast!

"Boy," Tom Florie said suddenly. "You three guys look like you saw a ghost!"

"No, not a ghost!" someone called. "A giant killer woodchuck!"

"No! A giant killer Saint Bernard!"

Peals of laughter pierced the spring air.

"Okay, class," Miss Espinoza said. "Settle down. Let's cross!"

Jimmy, Janice, and William hesitated, still looking down the bridle path after Angelina. Finally, Janice shook her head.

"She's bluffing."

"Yeah," Jimmy said with a nod. "No way any pods hit Earth."

"Right," William said. "No way."

But as Miss Espinoza corralled the class toward the park exit, the three friends exchanged a worried glance. Then they ran—not across the street, but down the bridle path. After all, it was fast becoming a spring day, just after a frost—the ideal conditions for pod-to-chuck conversion.

Long division could wait.

DAN ELISH has written many books for both children and adults. His middle-grade novels *Born Too Short* and *The Worldwide Dessert Contest* have received rave reviews both on Earth and on Grindlepick. When he's not traveling throughout the galaxy for book signings, Dan Elish spends time with his wife and two children in New York City. He's never seen a frozen woodchuck emerge from Central Park but has installed chuckproof windows in his apartment, just in case. He suggests you do the same. www.danelish.com